THE SECRET OF THE KNOT GARDEN

THE SECRET OF
The Knot Garden

by

Diana Harker

Illustrations
by
Jonathan Harker

TABB HOUSE

First published in Great Britain 1989
Tabb House, 7 Church Street, Padstow, Cornwall, PL28 8BG

ISBN 0 90718 69 6

Typeset by St. George Typesetting, Redruth
Printed and Bound by Bookcraft Ltd., Midsomer Norton

FOR MY FAMILY

AND

CHARLIE AND DOROTHY SWIFT

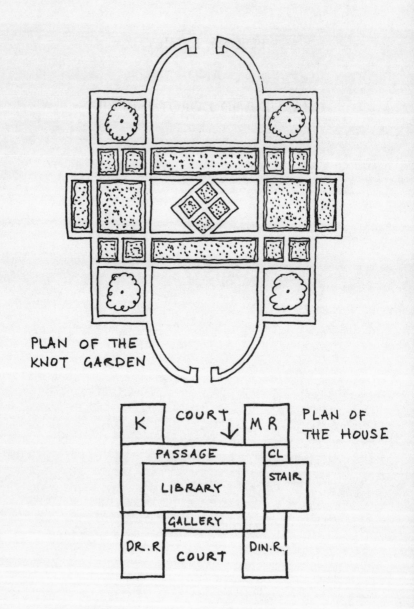

PLAN OF THE
KNOT GARDEN

PLAN OF
THE HOUSE

K	COURT ↓	M R
PASSAGE		CL
LIBRARY		STAIR
	GALLERY	
DR.R	COURT	DIN.R

CONTENTS

		Page
Map of the knot garden		vi
Prologue		ix
Map of Barton		x
Chapter		
1	Snipe goes missing	1
2	A long way from home	12
3	It's haunted, isn't it?	25
4	A nun's story	34
5	The man from the Ministry	44
6	Sanctuary	52
7	A scrap of silk	60
8	The same strange notes	71
9	'The creeping tide came up along the sand'	84
10	Letter from the past	96
11	The secret of the knot garden	107
12	The night of the concert	115
13	The figure in black	125
14	Safely across the Atlantic	131

PROLOGUE

There was no moon that night. Over the surrounding countryside the mournful sound of the air-raid siren rose and fell with a dreadful familiarity, fading away at last while villagers hurried to the safety of their cellars or shelters. The searchlights picked out the Heinkels flying low over the marsh and village on their way to bomb the port of Liverpool. There were seven planes in all . . . but the first one had already vanished from sight; no one saw the parachute drop softly or the figure that landed in a field, to disappear shortly in a clump of trees . . .

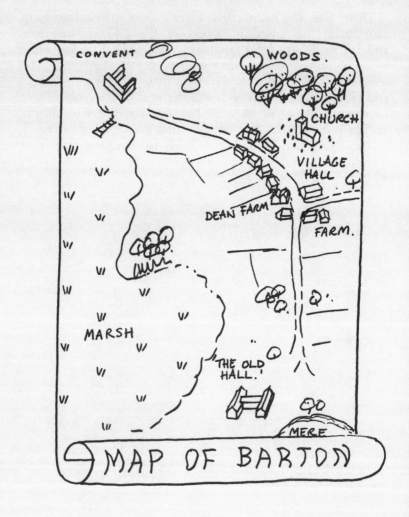

MAP OF BARTON

CHAPTER ONE

Snipe goes missing

IT wasn't that Aunt Mabel was unkind or even mean really, Dip thought, as he sucked hard on a juicy piece of grass, but that she seemed to turn home into an alien place whenever she took over. She was strict about meal times, incredibly tidy and her own special brand of furniture polish, which she used efficiently on every possible surface, made the whole house smell of disinfectant and beeswax – not a pleasant smell – reminding Dip of school after the holidays.

Not only that, but Peter played up when their mother was away – whining more, and reverting to sucking his thumb; acting more like a two or three year old instead of eight, which he was. Instead of being brisk with him, as she tended to be with Dip, Aunt Mabel seemed to revel in his behaviour – patting his curly hair and giving him little treats like scraping the bowl after she had made a sponge cake.

Up in the warm, sweet-smelling hay loft of Church Farm, Dip shifted his position and looked out over Three-acre meadow. Even the farm belonging to the Grants, which he had always known, seemed to have changed – that wasn't due to Aunt Mabel, but to the war. There were fewer cows, more land had been laid out for growing vegetables and two land girls had replaced the Grants' sons when they were called up.

One of them, Sylvia, spotted Dip as she strode over to the milking parlour. "Hey! What are you doing up there? Come down at once or I'll give you what for! I know all about little tykes like you – got three brothers of my own!" she shouted in a shrill Cockney voice, which sounded strange to Dip's ears, accustomed to more northern accents. "You'll be setting the plice on fire next!"

1

'Does she think I'm smoking up here or something?'
Dip wondered. It was unlikely, with cigarettes so scarce.
Nevertheless, he shinned down the ladder and reached the
door of the barn in time to see Sylvia turn on her heel and
toss her improbably brassy curls, which were barely restrained
by the land girl's hat perched on the back of her head.

The May evening was warm and sunny. It was Friday, and
with the week-end to look forward to, Dip decided to leave
his homework until Sunday evening. A cuckoo flew nearby,
calling loudly and clearly. Normally he would have felt more
cheerful but, apart from Aunt Mabel's arrival a few days ago,
it had been a blow when he realised that he wouldn't be
accompanying his mother to Portsmouth to see his father, a
sub-lieutenant in the Navy, while he was on embarkation leave.

"You must stay and look after Peter and our home," his
mother had said. "Aunt Mabel will rely on you to be the man
of the house – after all you're nearly twelve!"

Dip hadn't made too much fuss – he knew his mother was
looking forward to those few days. He really missed having Dad
around the place – it seemed to get worse as time went on.
When the war had started three years earlier he had thought
it couldn't last more than a few months – but now it felt as
if it had been going on for ever.

He dragged his feet up Shottington Lane towards home.
Macaroni cheese for supper tonight; well that was one bright
spot on the horizon. Aunt Mabel was a stickler for routine and
organisation, perhaps due to her spell as a games and gym
mistress at a girls' school in Dumfries many years ago. Now
she lived with her sister, Jeanie, and the two of them looked
after their very elderly father. Her menu never varied: boiled
eggs on Monday; sausages, if available, Tuesday; corned beef
hash or vegetable pie on Wednesday; fish or eggs – pickled,
poached or scrambled on Thursday; and macaroni cheese on
Friday. The meat ration was hoarded until the week-end and
was eked out by home-grown vegetables and rounded off by a
large fruit pie. Aunt Mabel was a good, careful manager, even
if she lacked imagination.

Dip had arranged to meet his friend, Tony, up in the hay loft.
It was a favourite meeting place with good views over Barton
woods, the village and marshes, and they enjoyed watching the

Home Guard setting off on manoeuvres, defending the gun emplacement in Shottington Lane or just drilling behind the village hall. Tony hadn't turned up this evening, however, and Dip decided to go round to his house after supper.

"Is that you, David?" Aunt Mabel's thin Scottish tones rang out. "You know I like to have high tea prompt at six o'clock. Hurry up now and wash your hands."

She always called him David and sometimes when she was angry used all his christian names – David Ian Philip. High tea at Dean Farm was taken in the sitting room where the Sinclairs lived. It was an old sandstone house, small and square and had been built in the seventeenth century. It was no longer a farm, the major part of the land having been sold off some years previously, but Mr Sinclair used the barns for the small building business which he had just been launching when the war broke out.

The dining-room was out of action now because it had been reinforced by wooden props to make sure it wouldn't collapse into the cellar if the house was hit by a bomb. The cellar was now used as an air-raid shelter by the family. Peter was already sitting at the table waiting for his macaroni cheese, his curly head bent expectantly over his plate, his long eyelashes, which frequently caused elderly women to exclaim, sweeping his pink and white cheeks and giving him the look of a saintly cherub.

Dip's own looks were more homely – straight, even lank, light brown hair, grey-brown eyes and a pale skin gave him an almost nondescript appearance until he smiled, when his whole face lit up.

Aunt Mabel's macaroni cheese was one of the best things she made and the three of them tucked into it with relish.

"Will you have some chutney with it?" Aunt Mabel pushed a large pot of her home-made gooseberry chutney towards the boys.

"No thank you." Dip loathed the stuff – it practically took the roof off the top of his mouth, making him gasp and his eyes water.

"Thanks," said Peter, who had acquired a taste for it. Aunt Mabel gazed at him fondly.

"You know a good thing when you taste it, don't you, Peter? I had a very good recipe for carrot cake today from Miss

3

Nightingale at the WI. I might try it this weekend. She told me she had heard from Mrs Plant that they're having evacuees at Shottington Hall. Eight billeted on them! Just think of that – and at a minute's notice too! Och that puir woman!''

Aunt Mabel's visits to Barton were infrequent but she usually managed to get back into village life as soon as she arrived – enjoying a gossip in the butcher's and attending church. She also had a gift for remembering everyone and their children's names as well as all their circumstances, which was useful. Now she was feeling indignant on behalf of the Ware-Gillows, who lived at Shottington Hall.

''Well, *I* think it'll make the place more homely,'' said Dip with his mouth full of bread and margarine; ''all those satin cushions and shiny bits of furniture – it never looks as if anyone really lived there.''

''They'll *ruin* the place.'' Aunt Mabel shuddered at the thought. ''Just think of the velvet curtains and that beautiful Axminster carpeting. I remember it all so vividly from my last visit. There was a musical coffee evening held there to raise money for Merchant Navy comforts . . .''

''With musical coffee being served I suppose,'' Dip muttered under his breath.

''How long have the Ware-Gillows been at the Hall?'' asked Aunt Mabel, pouring herself another cup of tea. ''I seem to remember a very elderly gentleman living there before the war . . . Colonel Sayer, wasn't it?''

''Yes, old Colonel Sayer – his family lived at the Hall for four hundred years. When he died, everything was sold up. Dad says the Ware-Gillows paid £11,000 for the Hall – he went to the auction.''

''That's a great deal of money,'' Aunt Mabel mused.

''Dad said he made his fortune in Huxley's Jam Doughnuts,'' Dip explained.

Peter had meanwhile been helping himself to the remains of the macaroni. Dip now made a grab for it but Aunt Mabel slapped him smartly on the wrist.

''First come, first served!'' She said briskly. She was full of these boring little sayings – 'little birds in their nest must agree', 'too many cooks spoil the broth', 'a rolling stone gathers no moss', 'manners maketh man', etc., but they never

4

seemed to work out to Dip's advantage. Peter smiled smugly.

"I'm going round to see Tony," Dip announced, pushing his chair back.

"You'll do no such thing until you've helped with the dishes, and what about your homework?"

"It's only a few old sums – I needn't do them till Sunday night," Dip said sullenly.

"I want to come with you to Tony's – I want to see his puppy," Peter whined.

"No, I want you to help me wind some wool and then I'll read you another chapter from *With Rod and Gun through darkest Basutoland.* That will be nice, won't it?"

Peter sighed – it was sometimes rather hard being Aunt Mabel's favourite – it wasn't all a bed of roses (as she might have said herself). Dip made a face at his brother in retaliation.

The dishes were soon dealt with and the table was laid ready for breakfast the next morning. Aunt Mabel settled in the squashy armchair by the open windows with her wool and a thick volume. On the cover was a picture of a grim-looking man clutching a rifle. He wore a bush hat shading a pair of stern eyes. She signalled to Peter to sit beside her.

*   *   *

TONY SWIFT lived at Sunny Corner with his mother and grandfather, whose chief interest in life was the eight hens they kept and a pig called Daisy. Tony's father was in the RAF – in Egypt at the moment, seeing for himself some of the places he had taught about in geography, before the war, at Weston Grammar School.

"Down, Snipe, down," Dip could hear Tony trying to train his new dog in the back garden. "Sit, there's a good boy, *sit!* Oh, hi," he called, as he caught sight of his friend coming through the side gate. "Sorry I couldn't meet you earlier, but one of Grandpa's hens escaped and flew up into a tree and I had to give a hand catching her. Luckily Snipe didn't make any effort to chase her."

By the sound of his name, Snipe should have been a thin little dog with a mean expression, but in fact was quite the opposite – a cross between a corgi and a labrador, he was

5

plump and amiable with a pair of bright, friendly eyes. He had arrived at Sunny Corner the previous week-end, brought along as a last hope by a distraught friend of Tony's mother's who had wanted a small lap-dog and couldn't cope with Snipe's abundant energy.

"I've taught him to sit – look. *Sit,* boy, sit!" Snipe wagged his tail and jumped up at Dip. "Sit." Tony pressed hard on Snipe's hind quarters and at last he got the message. Tony gave him a piece of bread.

"Grandpa gave me this," he went on, taking out of his pocket what looked like a whistle. He blew hard on it and his round, dark eyes were full of amusement as no sound came out. "It's a silent dog whistle," he explained, "inaudible to the human ear. I thought we'd take Snipe for a walk, and try it out."

"OK. Where shall we go?"

"We could go down to the marsh and hide behind the pill-box," Tony suggested.

"I've got a better idea. Let's go to Shottington Hall – we could go down by the mere – there are plenty of trees and reeds to hide behind there. Besides, I've just heard they're expecting dozens of evacuees at the Hall any minute. Perhaps they've arrived already. If they're anything like the ones from Bootle who were dumped on the Vicarage, we should be in for a bit of fun!"

"That lot only stayed about three weeks." Tony grinned, remembering the fights they'd all enjoyed, and the hidden dens and traps they'd made up in Barton Woods. It had seemed quite flat when the children had been transferred to a safer hamlet in North Wales, to the everlasting relief of Miss Truce, the vicar's sister.

"We're quite near Liverpool, as the crow flies," Dip remarked. "It seems funny to send evacuees here – we have quite a number of air-raid warnings. And look at all the shelters we have in the village."

"Yes, but it's safer than Wallasey or Bootle – we've only had one bomb land anywhere near and we're round the corner on the River Dee, not the Mersey, which is what the bombers are aiming at with the port and all the ships."

"Only one bomb has *officially* landed near, and that was

6

really a land mine, but what about that one they say landed up in the woods *and* the one in the spinney by Shottington Hall – both unexploded and likely to go off at any time? We could even be taking a terrible risk just going anywhere near the Hall,'' he added mournfully.

"Oh, those are just rumours.'' Tony dismissed the unexploded bombs with a shrug.

"No smoke without fire,'' Dip said darkly, quoting one of Aunt Mabel's favourite maxims. "And what about that story of . . .''

"Come on, let's move.'' Tony fetched Snipe's lead in case they met any sheep and catching sight of it, the dog went wild with excitement.

The trees down Shottington Lane were shady and overhung the road. The old signpost pointing south and saying 'Shottington 1 mile' had been removed as a precaution in case enemy troops landed, as had others along the main road to Chester and Liverpool. Where the Church Farm pig-sties used to stand, there was now a gun emplacement used by the Home Guard.

The two boys kicked a stone across the lane to each other as they went along – there was very little traffic on the road nowadays, just the odd bike, sometimes a horse and cart, very occasionally a car and about twice a day at irregular times, the local bus.

Dip gave the stone a particularly vicious kick and it went further than he had intended – through a sparse beech hedge, where it landed on something metallic. There was a cry of anger.

"What the blazes!'' A furious thin white face, topped by a shock of red hair, glared over the top. It was Eric 'Clanger' Bulley, seventeen years old – too young to be called up and in the meantime taking his Home Guard duties very seriously. These and his church duties, keeping the churchyard tidy, tending the precarious heating system in the winter and helping on a milk delivery round kept him busy, but the real joy had gone out of his life the day Mr Truce the vicar told them that the church bells would not be rung while the war was on – unless it was to announce an invasion. The pleasures of being a ringer on those Sunday mornings – the cacophony of

7

noise, triumphant and jubilant or more restrained according to the occasion, the refreshing drinks of cider after bell practice – had all come to an abrupt stop until the war ended. The only consolation was the vicar's promise that Eric and his fellow campanologists should announce the peace, when it came, in their own special way. Eric lived for the day – he would make sure they rang a peel such as had never been heard before!

He had been busy polishing his rifle ready for drill that evening, when the stone landed on it giving him a nasty shock.

"What d'you think you're doing then? Trying to be clever or something?" he growled.

"Sorry," Dip called back over his shoulder with exaggerated politeness.

Eric shook a wiry fist and muttered to himself, inspecting the butt. As he suspected, there was a small mark which hadn't been there before.

Dip and Tony, meanwhile, whistled, argued and joked their way along the lane until they came to a wooden gate at the bottom of the hill just before the village.

Tony stopped in the middle of an impersonation of the vicar's sister singing 'Rock of Ages' and said "Let's cut over here."

On the gate was a sign saying 'Trespassers Will Be Prosecuted' but they ignored it and, making sure no one was around, Tony hauled over the struggling Snipe and they were soon scrambling along the side of the hawthorn hedge towards a spinney.

The farm land of Shottington Hall estate extended to 300 acres and was separated from the gardens by a ha-ha, which was a sloping ditch of four to five feet deep which kept the animals out, but at the same time did not obstruct the view from the Hall.

The boys reached the spinney and plunged into the undergrowth. They crawled along on their hands and knees until Dip suddenly shouted in a hoarse whisper, "Look at that!" A great pile of twisted barbed wire loomed up in front of them blocking their way. "It must be to mark the unexploded bomb," Dip guessed, turning pale.

"Course it isn't," Tony reassured him – "It's probably just been dumped there to get it out of the way – or to stop German tanks in case of invasion."

8

"Well, I'm not going any further this way," Dip said firmly.
"Oh, come *on*."
But Dip wouldn't budge.
"Well let's crawl along the ha-ha – we can get to the mere that way; but keep down or we'll be in full view from the house."
They retraced their steps and wriggled along the bottom of the ditch until they could see a clump of white rhododendrons up above. Using them as shelter, the boys climbed out to get a quick glimpse of the Hall. It was a strange old building, dating from Tudor times – two side wings, one pebble-dashed in the last century, the other, a warm-coloured brick, were joined by an attractive black and white cross wing with overhanging eaves and gallery. The courtyard was cobbled. Virginia creeper and ivy now clung to the pebble-dashing and softened it a little and soon white roses would be climbing up to reach the gallery. The entrance was in the east wing and french windows opened out of the large beamed dining-room in the west wing to give views across the lawns to the Dee marshes and the Welsh hills beyond.

The boys didn't stop to admire the Hall, but skirted the shrubs and bushes and found a narrow path which led down to the mere. It was dark and cool here. Dip could remember when the water had frozen one severe winter years ago. Colonel Sayer had given permission for everyone in the village to come and ice-skate. Little red lanterns had been set up round the edge when it started to get dark and two maids from the Hall had appeared with lots and lots of piping hot sausages and soup.

Dip's father had pulled him round on a small home-made sledge – he could remember the thick striped scarf he was wearing and the damp woolly feel of his gloves. Everyone had been happy and laughed even when they fell over.

To-day, it was very quiet, except for the quacking of some ornamental water fowl swimming round a patch of water lilies. Tall reeds had grown up, spreading insidiously now towards the middle of the mere and threatening to engulf it.

Tony remembered his dog whistle. "You take Snipe behind that tree and I'll go and hide and blow the whistle."

Snipe, however, wasn't in the least interested in the whistle, whether he heard it or not. He was more interested in the ducks and bounded away with excited yaps in their direction.

Tony's head appeared from behind a clump of reeds on the bank. "What d'you want to go and let him escape for? He'll probably end up slaughtering all those birds!" he shouted angrily.

"It wasn't my fault – I expect your special whistle drove him mad – he's probably foaming at the mouth by now!" They glared at each other.

"We'd better go after him, anyway," Tony said. The ducks had squawked as Snipe crashed towards them, but all was quiet now and he had apparently gone off on a more diverting scent.

They started calling his name, quietly at first but when that produced no results, loudly and desperately with piercing whistles. "Snipe, come here, boy!" "There's a good dog!" Getting no result, they dashed round the perimeter of the mere to the other side.

"He must have gone that way," Tony pointed to where the path ended in an archway made of mellow old brick leading to a formal garden of rose beds and lawn in front of the house.

"Oh, *no!*" groaned Dip. "How will we get him now? We'll have to go and knock at the door and explain."

"Look!" Tony grabbed Dip's arm suddenly. Through the arch they could see a young girl coming out of a door and into the cobbled courtyard. They watched while she walked out onto the lawn, pulled out an apple, which had been bulging in a cardigan pocket, and studied the cover of a book she was carrying.

"She must be one of the evacuees," Dip whispered. "I wonder where all the others are?" The girl walked aimlessly, dragging her feet. She looked both bored and unhappy, her pale face framed by dark brown curly hair.

"She's coming this way," Tony hissed. "If we attract her attention without anyone from the Hall seeing, perhaps she'll have a look round for Snipe for us."

"She *might*," Dip conceded, "but she might think . . ." At that moment the girl turned round, startled, as round the corner of the west wing of the Hall rushed a large black cat closely followed by Snipe, barking joyously and looking very pleased with himself.

The boys yelled with one accord "Snipe!", but their delight

10

only lasted a second. They were seized roughly from behind by a very strong pair of hands.

CHAPTER TWO

A long way from home

JOANNA PALMER had only arrived at Shottington Hall just before tea. The train on which she travelled up from London had arrived at Chester station an hour late. It had been a tiring and miserable journey and she knew that at the end of it she would have to say goodbye to Mackie – Miss Maclean – who had looked after her for as long as she could remember, her mother having died when she was just a baby, eleven years ago.

Mackie's eyes looked suspiciously watery and her nose became scarlet – a familiar sign that she was worried or upset. Joanna clung to her, while the chauffeur from the Hall put her suitcase in the back of the large black limousine, and although she only said, in her rather brusque way, "Now, be a good girl and don't forget to write to me," Joanna knew that Mackie was feeling as upset as she was.

The drive to the Hall took twenty minutes and the chauffeur didn't seem to be the talkative type. Joanna caught a glimpse of a pair of cool grey eyes in the driving mirror. The eyes met hers and she looked away quickly, turning her attention to the surrounding country. They had come out of the City of Chester now, and were driving along a tree-lined road which crossed over a canal and went through a small village, passing the occasional inn and large stretches of rich farmland. To the left in the distance could be seen the hills of North Wales, appearing pale blue in the afternoon light.

It was all very different from Queen's Gardens, where she lived, in the heart of London. Even Hyde Park, where she used to go riding sometimes, was surrounded by impressive buildings and with traffic driving through, not like the real country.

A terrible wave of homesickness for the familiar tall house, where she had felt safe, despite the frequent air raids, came over her. She felt she might start crying at any moment and if she did, she knew she wouldn't be able to stop. In desperation she tapped the chauffeur's back. He was startled and jumped with alarm.

"I'm sorry, I just wondered if you could tell me how far Shottington is from Liverpool?"

For a moment or two, she thought he wasn't going to reply. Then he spoke slowly in a rather gruff voice. "Twelve miles."

"You see, my father is working there at the moment," Joanna went on, relieved to have some one to talk to. "That's why I'm here really – so as to be nearer him and I suppose it is safer than being in London. An aunt who lives in Canada wanted me to go out there and live with her, when the war broke out, but I would have hated that – although I could have had a pony and they ice-skate every winter on the frozen lake . . ." she broke off, aware that the chauffeur's eyes were scrutinising her. He seemed to unbend a little and, to her surprise, offered her a piece of chocolate, which he had broken off from a bar in his pocket. She took it gratefully; it seemed ages since she'd had any sweets, and her ration never lasted very long, but it tasted bitter.

"Your father, what does he do? Is he a cotton merchant perhaps?" he asked.

"Oh no, – nothing like that. He's a captain in the navy," Joanna said proudly, "and he's working on something important something to do with . . ." but she couldn't remember what it was her father had said on the telephone. He had been a bit vague about it and perhaps it was all 'hush hush'. She remembered seeing a poster at the library which read CARELESS TALK COST LIVES, so she decided to say nothing more.

At this moment, the car swung left between two small Victorian lodges. "Are we there?" Joanna asked, but the chauffeur had returned to silent contemplation, or perhaps thought the question too trivial to require an answer.

In spite of her unhappiness Joanna's spirits rose a little at the sight of the Hall – the mellow brick glowed warmly in the afternoon sun and the overhanging eaves looked sheltering. A large cedar tree stood protectively on the small front lawn and white doves were circling round making cooing noises.

The car scrunched to a halt on the gravel beside the open front door and Joanna got out. A severe-looking woman with dark hair drawn back in a bun, and wearing a brown print dress, appeared. "I suppose you must be Joanna; I'm Miss Jardine," she said brusquely. "Well, girl, fetch your case out."

Joanna struggled with the heavy case and lugged it into the dark hall while the car vanished round a curve in the drive beyond a belt of trees.

Miss Jardine was muttering as she walked along. "I hope you don't imagine we're going to wait on you hand and foot here, because if you do you've another think coming! Evacuees!" she said, darkly, half to herself, as she led the way. "Whatever next! I never expected this when I took the appointment – no indeed." She sniffed and said, more loudly, to Joanna, "Leave your case here; you'd better come and tell Mrs Ware-Gillow you've arrived."

The passage was dark and smelled pleasantly of lavender polish. Joanna dumped her case on the heavy pile carpet and Miss Jardine tapped at the oak door.

"Come in," said a distant voice.

"The evacuee, Madam," Miss Jardine announced grimly after they had entered the drawing room.

The room was flooded with sunlight and Joanna blinked for a moment or two, after the darkness of the hall and passage. The french windows were open wide and the pale green brocade curtains moved gently in the slight breeze.

By the fireplace the plump figure of a man dozed in a large wing armchair with a newspaper over his head which rose and fell in time with his gentle snores.

Afternoon tea was laid out on a small table by the french windows and a trolley bearing a silver tea set, plates of sandwiches, biscuits and small rock cakes stood nearby.

Edith Ware-Gillow, a comfortable-looking woman in her fifties, popped the remainder of a fish paste sandwich into her small rosily painted mouth and passed the plate of cakes to another woman who was sitting nearby.

"Do try one of these, Miss Linniment; Cook made them fresh this morning." Then, turning her ample frame with

14

difficulty, she peered at Joanna and beckoned with a chubby finger.

"Come over 'ere, child." To Miss Linniment, who was tucking into her cake with relish, with a linen napkin spread over her tweed skirt to catch the crumbs, she explained, "This is Joanna Palmer – a captain's daughter, you know – not an ordinary evacuee at all, of course. Her father's working in Liverpool – important government work – Top Secret." Here she raised finger to lip. "When Mrs Gutteridge asked if I'd take her so that she could be near her father, poor thing, I agreed at once, of course. I mean, we've all got to do our bit. I said to Josiah, who was dead against it, I said 'We'll all have to pull our weight now, Josiah,' I said."

The expression made Joanna suddenly want to giggle, looking at the considerable weight of Mrs Ware-Gillow. Instead, she fiddled with the shoulder strap of her gas mask and stood on one leg.

"Now run along with Miss Jardine and have a wash and tidy up. Then you can come and have a cup of tea in here. Only today, mind, as a special treat." She turned again to Miss Linniment. "I really don't know what things are coming to. Fancy having to have evacuees in our position and at our time of life." She shook her head of tight peroxided curls. "My nerves aren't what they were," she confided. Miss Linniment nodded her head sympathetically – wondering how she could get back to the topic of the church bazaar.

Miss Jardine, housekeeper at the Hall, walked ahead of Joanna, who was still struggling with her case. Back along the dark passage they went and into the hall. A wide oak staircase could be seen, dimly lit by a stained glass window. The beautiful carving on the balustrades was only just visible and the warm oak of the treads was almost completely concealed by garish multi-coloured carpeting. A crystal chandelier with gilt cherubs clinging to its centre looked out of place, but the dignity of the hall, stairs and landing was preserved by a small collection of oil paintings and portraits – some dating back to the Elizabethan period. There were handsome gentlemen with plumed hats, aloof young ladies with ringlets and silk dresses, old men in powdered wigs and one which particularly caught Joanna's eye, as they walked along the upstairs passage where

15

there was a little more light. This was an unusual portrait of a nun in a sombre black habit. The face which looked out from the white band of her wimple and severe head-dress, was, however, young and very pretty. Joanna paused, fascinated, but Miss Jardine rasped out "Come along – I haven't got all day. I've put you in here." She opened the door of a room which was small but looked comfortable.

"Thank you – it's very nice," Joanna said meekly.

"Hurry up and make yourself tidy and then you can go down to the drawing room. Normally, of course, when you come in from school, you will have your tea in the morning room." And with that she was gone.

School! Joanna shuddered. It was a frightening thought, especially going to a new one; a convent too, and she wasn't even a Catholic.

The patterned carpet from the stairs had continued down the passage and into her bedroom. The walls were covered in a floral wallpaper and the curtains were emblazoned with large yellow roses. The bedspread, however, was more subdued

16

and on it Joanna spied a letter and the sight of the familiar handwriting on the envelope made her heart leap. It was from her father. 'I'll save it for later, a special treat before I go to sleep,' she told herself as she put it carefully under her pillow.

She washed her hands and patted her hair in front of the mirror and stopped to gaze out of the small mullioned window which looked over lawns and farmland where cattle grazed contentedly. It was a lovely old house, and Joanna felt she could have been very happy there under different circumstances.

On her way down the passage, she paused again at the nun's portrait. It intrigued her – the wistful expression in the lovely clear blue eyes. She promised herself she would try to find out more about her, but just then she had to concentrate on finding her way back through the gloom to the drawing room.

Miss Linniment had vanished by this time and so had the small rock cakes, Joanna noticed. Mr Ware-Gillow had woken up and was drinking a cup of tea rather loudly. ''Oo's this then?'' He asked his wife, as he spied Joanna peeping round the door.

''Oh, there you are child, – I was wondering where you'd got to.'' Mrs Ware-Gillow gave a cross smile. ''This is Captain Palmer's daughter – the one I told you about. She's come to stay here for a short while.'' Her husband looked blank. ''Oh – you don't listen to a word I say, Joe. She's come from London while her father's working in Liverpool, Western Approaches – you know. Now sit down here,'' she said to Joanna, pointing to the sofa, with its carefully arranged satin cushions. Joanna sat down gingerly and was handed a small plate and linen napkin and a tiny knife. She felt all knees and elbows.

''Oh, we've run out of milk – just press that bell and Edwina can fetch us some more.'' Joanna did as she was asked and soon there was a knock at the door.

''Ah – Hedwina – we happear to be out of milk,'' and Mrs Ware-Gillow handed the silver jug to a young and rather glamourous-looking maid in a smart pink uniform and white apron. The front part of her auburn hair had been painstakingly arranged in a stiff pompadour which effectively concealed the starched white cap behind it. She peered into the jug. ''Yes – right out of milk,'' she pronounced.

Mrs Ware-Gillow looked at her suspiciously. This Edwina was apt to be a bit on the cheeky side given half a chance – a good natured girl but what she'd call saucy. It all came, no doubt, of having a name like Edwina – enough to give anyone ideas!

"Well, fetch us some more and be quick about it." Edwina caught Joanna's eye and winked as she went off to the kitchen.

When they were settled with fresh cups of tea and sandwiches, Mrs Ware-Gillow sat back and surveyed Joanna. "We'll have to do something about your 'air – it looks a right mess. Perhaps Miss Jardine could tie it all back with a ribbon or something. They're very strict at the convent you know. Your father's made all the arrangements and I rang them up myself only yesterday to say you'd be starting on Monday. Sister Teresa promised to arrange about the uniform when you get there. They have a second-hand shop at the school. You'll be the only day girl – they're making a special exception in your case."

Joanna's heart sank. Not only was she the only day girl but she had no uniform as yet and the term must have started two or three weeks ago. She'd stand out like a sore thumb.

"Do I have to go to this school?" she asked, adding desperately "I'm not a Catholic – I won't understand any of the things they do – the prayers and the beads," she said vaguely. "Isn't there another school I could go to or couldn't I stay off school for this term and work here with some books?"

Mrs Ware-Gillow had been unprepared for this sudden outburst. She was unused to children and shuddered at the idea of having a child around the house all day underfoot, cluttering up the place.

"Please," Joanna pleaded; "after all, I won't be here for very long so it's not really worth starting a completely new school and . . ."

Mrs Ware-Gillow drew herself up like a battleship; she glanced at her husband for some support but he had dozed off again.

"Well, I never heard of such a thing – not go to school? The very idea – and after all the trouble your father has gone to, to make all the arrangements – you don't seem to happreciate the fact that they're only fitting you in as a great favour. The Sacred 'eart comes 'ighly recommended." Her aitches had gone to pieces with this outburst and the colour had risen in her cheeks. She put her hand to her forehead – she could feel one of her headaches coming on. Really, it was too bad, the child had only been in the house about an hour and her nerves were already in shreds. This was what came of trying to help people.

"Hime going to my room now," she said, rising with dignity, "to 'ave a lay down, and I don't want to hear hanother word about not going to school." With which parting shot she swept out.

Joanna was left with Mr Ware-Gillow, who was snoring gently again now. She'd never felt so alone in her life. Her throat felt chokey and tears started pouring down her cheeks and wouldn't stop. She buried her head in one of the satin cushions and sobbed.

"Here, whatever's the matter with you? That'll never do – you'll ruin her ladyship's cushions," a voice said softly nearby. Joanna looked up through blurred eyes to see Edwina with a tray coming to clear the tea things away.

"Feeling a bit homesick are you?" She asked gently and put an arm round Joanna's heaving shoulders. "Look – give me a hand with this tray and then you can come down to the kitchen with me. I put a couple of those little cakes away in a tin."

They crept out of the room together and closed the door softly behind them. Along the passage and down a few steps was a green baize door and behind this lay the kitchen, a small sitting room, butler's pantry, larder, broom cupboards and a room devoted to washing, airing and ironing. The rooms were on the north side of the house and only caught the sun for a short while in the morning. Now they were quite dark but a small fire glowed in the sitting room and there were two or three comfortable old armchairs round the hearth. An oval table in the middle was covered in a brown cloth. A magazine called *True Love Stories* lay on top of the wireless together with a piece of yellow knitting and a tin with a picture of a thatched cottage on the lid.

"Here we are!" Edwina took up the tin and opened it, offering a small rock cake to Joanna. "Make yourself comfy."

Joanna sat back in front of the fire in one of the armchairs whilst Edwina helped herself to a cake. "I expect you're feeling a bit down in the mouth, eh? Away from home for the first time – only natural. I remember feeling exactly the same when I came here although I only live at Portgate – about six miles away. You're from London aren't you?''

Joanna nodded.

''I've always fancied going to London myself – I was thinking of getting a job as a waitress in one of those posh hotels. Of course, I shall be called up soon.''

''What are you going to join?'' asked Joanna.

''Oh, the WAAF. – All those good looking airmen, and I think the blue uniform will suit me, don't you?'' Edwina studied herself in the mirror over the mantelpiece. ''That blue cap – with the peak. Perhaps I shall put my hair up like Betty Grable in her last film.''

Joanna was feeling a little better now. ''I don't suppose you get many raids here,'' she said.

''Oh – we get our fair share – the German planes pass over on their way to Liverpool but of course we don't get many bombs actually falling here, although we've had the odd one or two,'' Edwina replied.

"My father's in Liverpool; I hope he's safe." Joanna suddenly felt upset again.

"Safe as houses," Edwina said quickly; "they have special shelters for VIPs. They're right down under the City." She had heard from Cook that Joanna's father was high up in the navy, concerned with some top secret war work.

"And talking of shelters – just you wait till you see the one here – you've never seen anything like it. Cook and the rest of us just go down to the cellars but Mr Ware-Gillow has had this dugout built in the garden near the old tennis court. Well – they've got everything down there, talk about posh!" 'Posh' seemed to be Edwina's favourite word.

"Does it have satin cushions?" Joanna asked and they both laughed.

A shadow passed across the window. "That'll be Moses Jones coming for his mug of tea and I haven't put the kettle on yet." Edwina jumped up and patted the stiff quiff of hair to make sure it was still in position.

"Who's Moses Jones?" whispered Joanna.

"You've met him already – he brought you here in the car this afternoon – he's chauffeur, odd-job man and gamekeeper all rolled into one bundle of Welsh charm." Remembering his rather grim expression and stern eyes, Joanna doubted if Edwina meant the last part.

"I've got all the vegetables to do for dinner tonight as well – it's Cook's afternoon off," Edwina explained as she started bustling about.

"I suppose I'd better go and unpack," Joanna said. There was no Mackie to do it for her; but she was unwilling to leave the warm and friendly atmosphere.

"Yes, love, you go and do that. We'll have a drink of cocoa together before you go to bed," Edwina promised, then she turned to address Moses Jones who had opened the back door. "Don't forget to wipe those boots," she shouted, "I scrubbed the floor this afternoon. Look at your boots," she shrilled, pointing at them.

"Oh – yes indeed!" He scraped the soil off them and rubbed them on the mat. His chauffeur's peaked cap had now been replaced by a rough tweed one, which Joanna supposed must be his gamekeeper's uniform. She wondered if he had a special one for when he was the odd job man. She left the kitchen reluctantly and found her way back upstairs to her bedroom.

As she opened the door, a shaft of late afternoon sunlight illuminated the nun's portrait in the passage. 'She's very beautiful,' Joanna thought again. 'Too pretty and young to be a nun.' She had somehow imagined all monks and nuns to be elderly and very plain. If some of the ones at the convent were like this, perhaps it wouldn't be such a bad place after all. Down in the bottom right hand corner of the painting was the name of the artist written very faintly. Joanna peered closely – it looked like Thomas Argyle. The nun appeared to be carrying a prayer book, and entwined in her elegant fingers was a crucifix and chain of a distinctive style – the cross encrusted with rubies. She was standing against the background of a summer garden with clipped hedges. When Joanna went into her room and looked back, the blue eyes of the portrait seemed to follow her.

There wasn't much unpacking to do and Joanna had soon stuffed her clothes and belongings into the small wardrobe and dressing table. Jumbo, a moth-eaten grey fur elephant sporting a striped blue and green tie, was placed lovingly on her bed.

She wondered what to do next. It was unusually quiet. No sounds came from the house and the grounds and surrounding countryside were still and peaceful, apart from the birds. Joanna was used to the sounds of London: bustling life going on in the streets – the noises of the traffic and constant streams of people rushing about busily.

This silence seemed unnatural. She started to hum a tune and opened the door of her bedroom again – she wasn't even able to slam the door behind her with a reassuring bang, because of the thick carpet. Nor could she even hear her own footsteps walking along the landing and down the stairs.

She decided to look round the rest of the house and get to know her way about. Opening a door opposite the front entrance, she found herself in the dining room. The Ware-Gillows had obviously been at work here. The carpet was of an even more intense pattern – to hide spilt gravy or crumbs perhaps – the red and gold flock wall paper made the room dark and it appeared even more gloomy as one pair of red plush curtains had been drawn to protect the veneer on the reproduction regency table, on which sat much silver plate

22

– candles, tureens and a large ornate punch bowl.

There was a rather stale smell of cigar smoke and strong cheese. Joanna shut the door and went out into the corridor again. A cloakroom was on the left and a small cheerless room containing a small table, four chairs, a modern sideboard and a desk overflowing with papers. The morning room, she supposed, not looking forward to the lonely meals she'd be having there.

There was an arched oak door on the right which she'd noticed before. It was somehow different from the others – it looked older and there was a latch to lift up instead of a handle to turn. The door creaked as Joanna opened it, as if not many people had used it recently. It led into another room. This was the library – a room quite unlike all the others. It looked as if it had been untouched not only by the Ware-Gillows but by generations of previous owners. The lofty ceiling seemed to stretch right up into the rafters of the roof. A narrow wooden staircase at one end of the room led up to a gallery where there were small arched windows and bookshelves full of brown leather-bound volumes. There were also book-cases at ground-floor level, a tapestry, portraits, a pair of library steps, more windows and a stout oak door leading to the courtyard. At the opposite end of the room to the staircase, the wall was empty apart from a large religious painting placed between two niches. The floor in here was uncarpeted – thick wide wooden boards echoed Joanna's footsteps as she walked across the room. She now saw that the wall, the colour of parchment, was covered in old decorated plasterwork. A frieze of flowers and beasts ran above and below the painting and to look more closely she had to go up a step on to a slightly higher level. On closer inspection, both panels of plasterwork appeared to represent the story of Adam and Eve and the garden of Eden, with plants and animals surrounding a large tree in the middle and two small primitive figures below. Joanna thought it was more like a church than a library, but she was excited by this unusual room.

She walked over to look at some of the titles of the books. There were not many she recognised apart from a set of Walter Scott's Waverley Novels and *Pilgrims Progress*. Near a collection of books on ancient history were three volumes of *The History of Cheshire*.

Joanna took one down. It was covered in dust and smelt very musty and she suddenly longed for a breath of fresh air. The thick door leading to the courtyard was bolted but with a little effort she managed to ease the bolt back. It was wonderful to smell a mixture of freshly mown grass and wallflowers. She stepped over the cobbles of the courtyard and looked back at the library. This part of the house had been left in its original black and white timbered state and the remains of an outside gallery, at the same level as the inside one, clung to the wall.

Joanna opened the book and wandered over to the lawn. In her pocket, she discovered a small apple that Mackie had given her that morning for the train journey. It seemed days ago already. The book looked uninteresting. The print was very small and there were no pictures.

Suddenly the peace and quiet of the evening was broken – as a sleek black cat streaked across the grass, followed in hot pursuit by a yapping dog. At the same moment, two very scruffy boys leapt out from behind a hedge and started shouting excitedly.

CHAPTER THREE

It's haunted, isn't it?

THE grip tightened cruelly on the two struggling boys and a harsh voice rasped out "You – what you doing here?" They were shaken violently then dropped suddenly.

They turned to look at their assailant – a man of about thirty-five wearing a tweed cap under which glittered a pair of hostile grey eyes.

"We were only looking for our dog," Dip tried to explain, but was cut short.

"No trespassers," the man shouted in a gruff voice. "Now go and don't return – if I see you back here . . ." but words failed him at this point as if he couldn't think of any punishment bad enough.

"Phew," Tony said, as they reached the safety of the lane once more, "that's torn it. Snipe's gone and I don't know how we're going to find him. What shall we do? We can't leave him."

"Perhaps he'll find his own way home," Dip suggested unconvincingly; "and whatever is Aunt Mabel going to say when she sees all this?" He waved a hand eloquently over his torn trousers, filthy shirt, muddied shoes and socks. "She'll have a fit."

It was getting late. They whistled and called Snipe on the way back to the village but there was no sign of him. Upset and worried, they stopped May Cottrell the district nurse, who was cycling home from work, and begged her to look out for him. When they separated, they arranged to meet the following day and if Snipe hadn't turned up, to go and search for him.

*   *   *

THERE was an air raid warning that night. The siren sounded at half-past ten and the all clear didn't go until two o'clock. Aunt Mabel nevertheless insisted on them all rising as usual at 7.30, although it was a saturday. "Early to bed and early to rise," she muttered.

The novelty of spending half or all of the night down in the cellar had long since worn off. At first, Dip and Peter had been quite excited by the proceedings – putting on warm all-in-one siren suits when the wailing alarm was heard and creeping downstairs and then down the very old stone steps to the cellar in which some camp beds and a paraffin heater had been installed. Candles were used for light as there was no electricity down there and the flames would flicker, throwing shadows on the uneven stone ceiling while Dip's father told stories about his boyhood in Galloway – poaching in the lochs, exploring ruined castles and sharing great picnics up in the hills with all his cousins. Now and then a tin of precious sweets would be handed round. They hadn't noticed the slightly damp smell in those early days but now Aunt Mabel commented on it disparagingly while the boys, tossing around uncomfortably on rough blankets, felt both bored and apprehensive on hearing the German planes overhead and would imagine them being picked out by the searchlights on a gun-site at Shottington. They wonidererd how many Hurricanes or Spitfires would be coming out to retaliate.

Dip still felt half asleep as, having escaped Sylvia's eagle eye, he greeted Tony up in the hay loft after lunch. Neither had heard any news of the consequences of the raid. The information on the wireless was guarded.

"I've three pieces of news for you," Tony said. "The first – bad. No sign of Snipe; the second, funny; my mother heard it when she went to The Meet this morning." The Meet was the name given to the butcher's shop owned by the Martins in the village not only because it sounded like 'meat' but because the shop stood in the centre of the village where cottages clustered round a small green and where The Cheshire Hunt met regularly in peace-time. Also it was the natural meeting place for all the villagers, who swapped news and gossip while queuing for the weekly ration of meat or if they were lucky a little offal.

"The Martins," Tony went on, "slept so soundly in their cellar last night that they didn't hear the 'all clear' and when they woke this morning they could still hear the sound of the planes humming overhead and thought the raid was still on. It was so dark down there they didn't know what time it was. Someone had to shout down to them at nine o'clock this morning to open up the shop. It turns out that their heavy old refrigerator is over the cellar . . ."

"And makes a noise just like a squadron of bombers!" Dip interrupted, laughing. "What's the other piece of news?"

"Oh – that's very strange. Grandpa went out before the raid last night, looking for Snipe. He suddenly had the feeling that the dog might be wandering in the woods, where we've taken him for walks. Well, it was dark so he took a torch and as he got near the church, what do you think he heard?" Not pausing to give Dip a chance to reply, he hurried on, "Organ music – a strange haunting tune Grandpa said, with no proper beginning or ending and very high notes. He was still humming it this morning."

"Who was it then? It's not very unusual to hear organ music in church. Probably it was just Mr Bates practising for Sunday," Dip said.

"No, it couldn't have been. There were no hymns or anything like that, just this tune, out of the blue. Grandpa peered through the church door but there seemed to be no lights on and he couldn't see a thing. Just then the siren went and he had to hurry back home as quickly as he could."

"Perhaps it was mad Kate – her cottage isn't far from the church. Maybe she was out for an evening stroll with her cats and suddenly felt like playing a tune on the church organ."

"Well – perhaps," Tony replied doubtfully, "but the important thing now, is what are we going to do about Snipe? We'd better start in the direction of Shottington Hall and see how the land lies."

They climbed down from their perch and made their way along the Lane. Earlier, the boys had spied the Home Guard assembling at the back of the village hall and from their view point had watched them drilling. Now the whole platoon of The 21st Cheshire was marching down the lane in the direction of Shottington led by Eric Bulley – looking neither to left nor right and scowling with concentration. Reg Eccles, the sergeant, was in command and Bob Bevis and Bill Jellicoe, two veterans of the First World War, were bringing up the rear, with their rifles slung over their shoulders.

"Look at old Cat's-eyes Cox," Dip nudged Tony as they were overtaken. The pebble lenses of their form-master's spectacles glinted in the sun and he blinked as he tried unsuccessfully to march in time with the others. The boys marched after them with exaggerated swinging of the arms.

Coming to a stile on the right, the platoon suddenly veered off and, once in the field beyond, half the body of men started running one way and half the other.

"They must be on man-oeuvres – it's a shame we can't track them," said Dip.

"We've got to find Snipe first," Tony said firmly. "He might be caught in a trap or anything."

They soon found themselves back in the spinney belonging to Shottington Hall. Not wishing to come face to face with the gamekeeper, they crept along cautiously, keeping an eagle eye open for the dog, and now and giving again a blow on the silent dog whistle.

After about half an hour of searching they were skirting the other side of the mere when Dip gripped Tony's arm – "What's that?" he whispered.

A bush in front of him seemed to move and behind it, it looked as if two other small trees were following.

Dip sighed with relief as a pair of thick glasses peered out of the greenery of the 'bush'. "It's only Cat's-eyes."

Mr Cox seemed relieved to see the boys. "Is that you, David?

28

We seem to have – er – lost our way slightly – Could you point us in the direction of the marsh?"

Eric Bulley, covered in camouflage was obviously angry. "Thought you said you knew the way – we were relying on you. The others must have captured the gun emplacement by now while we've been wandering round here. We must have lost about twenty points," he muttered sullenly.

"Well, I think it's that way, sir," Tony said, trying to get his sense of direction. "You'll have to go along by the house and keep going straight on." He pointed to where he thought the marsh lay.

"Thank you, boys," Mr Cox shouted and the three of them made off – running and dropping pieces of greenery as they went.

A minute later there was an angry roar. Moses Jones had spotted them and was giving chase. The boys followed a little way behind and saw the figures disappearing in the distance.

"Quick, this could be our chance to scout round the outside of the house," Tony said quickly. "I bet you anything, Snipe is still somewhere round here."

They dashed across the lawn to the gravelled drive and found themselves near the garages, outhouses and the kitchen door into the Hall. They peered into what looked like a potting shed, with thick wooden work bench and tools hanging on hooks round the walls and plant pots stacked everywhere.

"Someone's coming!" Dip and Tony hid behind the door as they heard footsteps drawing near. They paused outside, and then came right in, followed by a clear voice calling out "I know you're in here – I saw you from upstairs."

The boys came out from behind the door and found themselves confronted by Joanna.

"I know why you're here too – you're looking for your dog. Well, he's quite safe; Edwina and I hid him in the log store."

"Where's that?" Tony asked. They were both so relieved and pleased to hear that Snipe was safe that their only thought was to retrieve him and get home as quickly as possible.

"Well don't say 'thank you'," Joanna scowled. 'We had a lot of trouble keeping him hidden after I found him wandering round yesterday evening. Moses Jones was absolutely furious."

She went on to explain how she had seen them being 'told off'.

They recognised her as the girl they had seen reading a book on the lawn and Tony muttered his thanks.

"He's in here," Joanna said. She led the way to the log store where, in the gloom, they could make out the form of the excited dog. Snipe was overjoyed to see the boys and started yelping with pleasure. "Shhh," Tony cautioned.

"I expect you're one of the evacuees," Dip said to Joanna. "Where are all the others?"

"What others?" Joanna asked, puzzled.

"We heard there were going to be about a dozen billeted here with the Ware-Gillows," he replied.

"Oh, I wish there were," Joanna sighed. "No – there's only me. I only arrived from London yesterday. There are only grown-ups around here. Edwina's nice, though."

"Who's Edwina?"

"She's a parlour maid – but she's not at all frightened of Miss Jardine and she's leaving soon to join the WAAF." Joanna's words tumbled out, she was so pleased to have someone of her own age to talk to.

"It must be awful living here with the Ware-Gillows," Dip sympathised; "all that velvet and satin and things – ugh! – The place is haunted – did you know that?" he asked, brightening a little at the thought.

"Who by?" asked Joanna. In the bright sunny afternoon she forgot, for the moment, that she would sometimes lie awake for hours remembering a frightening part of a book or a ghost story she'd heard on the wireless.

"Can't remember," said Dip frowning.

"My father is coming over to see me three weeks today. He would have come this week-end but he's had to go up to Scotland suddenly." Joanna touched the letter in her pocket. "He's a Naval Captain, based in Liverpool at the moment on secret war work," she added impressively.

Dip and Tony, not to be outdone, told her of their fathers' war exploits.

They were wandering round the back of the house now, with Snipe firmly on his lead. No one was around. The Ware-Gillows had gone to visit some friends and Moses Jones wouldn't be collecting them until six o'clock. Cook was lying down and Miss Jardine was sorting through the linen chest at the top of the house.

Joanna peered through the kitchen window. Edwina was putting the kettle on for an early afternoon cup of tea. She caught sight of the three children and beckoned them in.

The boys thanked her for hiding Snipe. "I gather Moses Jones wasn't too pleased when he caught you yesterday," she grinned. "Well, he has got rather a temper – haven't got used to it myself yet – he's only been here a short while. He suffered a mining accident in the Rhonda Valley and couldn't get employment there afterwards – walks with a bit of a limp. Perhaps it still hurts and that's what makes him cross."

A large batch of ginger biscuits lay on the table. "Go on, take one, Cook won't miss three. D'you want a glass of milk?" They chatted for a while, telling Edwina about Mr Cox losing his way.

"Moses keeps a few traps down by the mere and doesn't like them disturbed. Perhaps you'd better not stay too long; I expect when he's given the Home Guard a piece of his mind he'll be back here for his tea."

Snipe, who'd been tied up outside, was beginning to whine. "I'll come with you as far as the mere," Joanna said, reluctant to see them go, but before they'd crossed the lawn, Dip's sharp eyes spotted a distant figure coming from the direction of the marsh. It was wearing a tweed cap. "Dodge down," he warned.

"Follow me," Joanna whispered urgently, "I know where to hide". Concealed in a large rockery, the boys spied a small wooden door which Joanna now opened. Tugging Snipe, Tony followed her into the dark beyond. Dip closed the door behind them. On a shelf near the door, Joanna found a torch which she now switched on.

"It's the Ware-Gillow's air-raid shelter – their dug-out," she explained. "We came down here last night. They never lock it, in case they lose the key in an emergency. Come right in; I'll show you. I bet you've never seen a shelter like this before!"

She led the way down a steep flight of steps between high concrete walls to a stout door – again unlocked. Opening it, Joanna shone her torch around and located a large oil lamp standing on a table in the middle of the shelter. A box of matches lay nearby and soon the lamp was lit, giving out a bright and cosy light.

They looked around. The shelter was furnished as a comfortable bed-sitting room with every modern convenience. The boys were amazed. "Coo, look at those," said Dip, pointing to the bunk beds covered in leopard-skin rugs. "Did you sleep on one of those?" he asked Joanna.

"No, I used a camp bed. We made a cup of coffee though." She went over to a meat safe in the corner and opened it, showing all the provisions inside. There was a small wash basin, a primus stove, a kettle, magazines and a furry rug on the floor.

"We get fresh air from those two pipes – they lead up into the other side of the rockery. Mrs Ware-Gillow can't stand being closed in, she made a terrible fuss all the time we were down here. That's why they made it like a proper room, I think, so that she wouldn't feel so strange, but she can't get used to it. He just went straight to sleep and snored very loudly. She asked me to read aloud to her from some magazines – I don't think she was really listening but she said it 'soothed her nerves'. Then she went on about some of the food being missing.

"I'm sure there were height chocolate biscuits in this 'ere tin' '', Joanna said, in a good imitation of Mrs Ware-Gillow's voice.

"That sounds just like her," Dip laughed. "This would make a good den. Does anyone come here in the daytime?"

"No, of course not – only if there's a raid."

"You could come down here anytime then," Tony remarked.

"Well, it's not much fun on your own and besides I won't be free during the week, I've got to start at a dreadful school on Monday," Joanna pulled a face. "A convent."

"Not – *the* convent!" Dip and Tony made faces of mock horror.

"Do you know it then? Is it really terrible?" Joanna asked worriedly.

"Of course we know it – it's down on the marsh. The girls all go for walks on Sunday."

"Two by two," interrupted Tony.

"Wearing white gloves and blue hats," Dip continued, "with their eyes cast down."

32

"And with an old nun like a black raven keeping them all in order."

They walked sedately up and down the shelter taking tiny steps and collapsed, laughing, in a heap on the leopard-skin rug.

"It's all very well for you to joke," Joanna muttered.

Snipe was starting to get excited. "We'd better take him home – I wonder if the coast's clear now," Tony said.

They looked cautiously round the small door in the rockery and then crept out.

"Well, thanks again for looking after Snipe – I don't suppose your school will be all that bad," Tony said unconvincingly, feeling rather sorry for her.

Joanna watched wistfully as they went off in the direction of the mere.

Dip turned round. "I've just remembered something – all that talk about the convent reminded me – it's the ghost of a *nun* that haunts this place."

CHAPTER FOUR

A nun's story

JOANNA hated her new school, an old rambling grey building down on the marsh, with the constant sound of sea birds screeching as they wheeled overhead. When she came back to the Hall, she took her tea to eat in the kitchen for Edwina's company, whenever she could. The morning room was cold, cheerless and lonely. The walls were painted a depressing shade of dark green whereas the small sitting room by the kitchen was always snug and homely.

"But there must be some nice girls there," Edwina protested after Joanna had been at the convent for about a week.

"There aren't – there really aren't. Some of them seem friendly when the nuns are around but the minute they've turned their backs they start being horrible again – you know, teasing and sly, and look at my uniform – miles too big."

"Well, I do see what you mean." Edwina looked critically at the blazer which was at least two sizes too large.

"I've tried tucking the sleeves up but they just come down again. Sister Teresa said I was lucky to get one at all from the second hand shop and went on about clothing coupons but I'd rather have managed without; and my skirt feels as if it's falling down all the time." She sighed "And it's *awful* arriving each day driven by a chauffeur. Francesca Stewart says the Ware-Gillows must get their petrol on the black market. Do you think they do?"

"You'll have to ask Moses Jones about that, won't you? On second thoughts, perhaps you'd better not mention it – he might take it personally. Now how about another cup of tea?"

"Yes, I'd love one thank you . . . and I haven't told you, have I, that I'm the only one – the only one in the *whole*

34

school who doesn't attend mass – and I've got some dreadful homework to do tonight – all about the Civil War. All the others did it last term – I don't know anything about it . . .''

"You're a real old misery this evening, aren't you? You know you're bound to feel a bit strange at first – I did when I came here. Can't you think of one good thing about that school of yours?"

Joanna frowned and thought hard for a moment. "Well there's Sister Annunciata who's very nice – she's young and pretty and I think she comes from Austria although some of the girls say she's really from Germany. Anyway she seems a bit sad – I suppose she's far away from her homeland and family – and she's always kind to me and explains things. She reminds me a little of the nun in the portrait in the corridor by my room – you know the one I mean?"

"Yes – I know the one – she seems to smile when I flick the feather duster over her. As a matter of fact they say she haunts this place." Edwina stole a look at Joanna to see her reaction – at least a change of subject might help her to forget her woes for a while.

"Dip and Tony told me about the ghost of a nun at the Hall but somehow I never thought of it being that one," she said excitedly, "Do tell me the whole story – I really must know it!"

"Well, I can't remember all the details – Betty from the Lodge told me. My version will be a bit sketchy but it seems that her name was Alice and she was the daughter of Sir William Sayer. There was a war going on at the time – I think it was this Civil War you were talking about – anyway, the Sayers supported the King and Alice had fallen in love with someone on the opposite side. Well, there was a terrible row. Her father forbade her to see her young man ever again, so she decided to become a nun and went to a convent in France. But," Edwina paused for dramatic effect, "just before she was to take her final vows, she came home for the last time, and I suppose this was when she had her portrait painted, in her novice's habit and then, blow me, she vanished into thin air. Nobody knew where she went. Her father died soon after of a broken heart, they say. Some people thought she'd done away with herself but I wouldn't be surprised if her father hadn't locked her up in a secret room or something," Edwina was getting into her

35

stride now, "or even he might have *walled* her up!"

Joanna's eyes were round. "Why would he want to do that?"

"Ours is not to reason why! I expect he couldn't bear the thought of losing her either to the church or to the enemy." Edwina's voice had sunk to a low and melancholy tone.

"But what happened then . . .?"

"I told you, I don't know any of the details – but it would make a beautiful story for a film, wouldn't it?" Edwina went over to the mirror and draped her blue apron over her head in what she hoped was a nun-like manner but the effect was spoilt by a piece of auburn curl which kept escaping.

Joanna shivered. "Do you think she clanks round at midnight or just drifts silently from room to room passing between the walls?"

"Oh, I shouldn't think there's a word of truth in any of it so don't start worrying your head about that," Edwina said briskly. "You know how these old stories are just a load of nonsense half the time." She looked critically at Joanna. "If I've got a minute this weekend, I'll see what I can do with your blazer and skirt. We can't have you going around looking like an old scarecrow, can we? Especially as I happened to hear you may be having a certain visitor one day next week," she gave one of her winks – "but perhaps I shouldn't be saying anything."

"You mean my father?" Joanna's eyes shone. "When did you hear it?"

"Well, I just happened to be taking in some hot scones when Mrs Ware-Gillow was telling her hubby that Captain Palmer had telephoned to say he may be able to come over on Tuesday or Wednesday and . . ."

"That'll be wonderful!" Joanna shouted.

"But they weren't to tell you," Edwina went on, "in case he couldn't manage it at the last minute and you might be disappointed, so you'd better not let on I told you anything about it."

"No, I won't." Joanna popped a piece of hot buttered toast into her mouth, all thoughts of the ghost forgotten.

"Oh there you are, child." Mrs Ware-Gillow swept into the kitchen. "I've been looking for you heverywhere."

Joanna was surprised at this – she rarely saw either of the

Ware-Gillows except perhaps for five minutes or so in the evenings before she went to bed.

"I want you to do something for me. No, Hedwina, you get on with the silver – you know we have company for dinner this hevening." She had her large black sleek cat clutched to her ample chest. It was the same cat, Cleopatra, which Snipe had chased and which now stared round lazily while being stroked by white pudgy fingers, covered in rings.

"Come along with me, Joanna; I don't know what you're doing in 'ere hanyway – shouldn't you be doing your sums or something?" she asked vaguely.

She led the way through to the hall, talking all the while. Joanna thought she might mention her father's visit but Mrs Ware-Gillow's mind was on a concert the Women's Institute was planning to put on. "It's all in a good cause, although I can't remember exactly what, and they want some clothes for some songs they're doing – one from *The Mikado* by Gilbert and Sullivan and one called 'The Nun's Chorus'. I promised Miss Linniment a fan for the Chinese number and we have some spare blackout material which she said would come in nicely for the nuns' habits. Miss Jardine has sorted them out and one or two other bits and pieces and put them upstairs in one of the attics. But she's not back from Liverpool yet." She sighed and gave a little shrug. "Moses took her in to do some shopping, so I want you to run upstairs and find them all for me, and don't take long because Miss Linniment rang up just now to say she's sending two boys round to collect it all right away." She paused for breath and stroked Cleopatra, who showed signs of being restless. "And, by the way," she went on, "The Reverend Truce and his sister are coming for a bite to eat this evening – you'd better come in and be hintroduced at about half past seven and put a comb through you 'air first." With that she waddled off back to the drawing-room and Joanna ran up the stairs to the top of the house.

There was a maze of rooms up here. She'd been up only once before when Edwina showed her some of her family photographs she kept in her room, cosy with sloping ceilings and tiny windows. Miss Jardine's room and Cook's bedroom were also up here but further along the passage were lumber rooms, attics full of disused furniture and empty forgotten rooms.

Some of the doors that Joanna tried just opened into deep cupboards, but round the corner was a small attic which looked more promising. In it were piles of old curtains, stacks of books, faded photographs and a battered leather trunk with the initials 'G.W. de Q.S.' barely visible on top.

There was a small and ancient sewing machine on top of a card table by the window and yards of black material – some halfway through being stitched. Miss Jardine had evidently been making a start on one or two of the nuns' habits. A large pile of the material lay on the floor near the trunk and a small piece of black fabric hung out of one corner of it.

'This must be it,' Joanna thought and went to gather it up but stopped as she heard footsteps approaching along the uncarpeted corridor. She peered round the door. "Oh it's you," she said, pleased to see that it was Dip and Tony who'd come looking for her.

"We've been sent up to get the material. It looks as if you've found it," said Tony pointing to the pile on the floor.

"That's some of it – we'd better leave the pieces by the sewing machine, oh and it looks as if there might be some more in that old trunk."

They folded it up as best they could and then Dip undid the leather straps that bound the trunk. They were stiff and unyielding. "It doesn't look as if this has been opened for years." He gave a final strong tug and one of the straps loosened. Tony managed to heave the other one free of its buckle, and they pushed back the lid and peered in.

A jumble of papers met their eyes. The black material which had stuck out of the end turned out to be a small fragment of satin wrapped round some yellowing documents.

"Just some boring old papers," Dip said. Joanna picked up a sheaf of them that were covered in tiny old fashioned handwriting, and studied one for a moment. "It looks like some sort of attempt to write a history of The Sayer family. That would account for the initial 'S' on the trunk."

"Old Colonel Sayer used to live in this house, so I suppose a lot of stuff was left behind after the sale and got dumped up here. I don't expect the Ware-Gillows have even been up in this part of the house." Dip closed the lid after Joanna had replaced the papers.

"That ghost of a nun you were talking about – that was her name too – Alice Sayer," Joanna said.

"How did you find that out?" Tony asked.

Joanna retold Edwina's story. The afternoon sun had vanished behind a dark cloud and the small room became gloomy and oppressive – "and she was never seen again," she concluded in a hushed tone of voice.

"It all sounds a bit far fetched to me," Dip said scornfully; "there probably wasn't any such person anyway."

"Yes there was," Joanna retorted. "I'll show you her portrait downstairs and . . ." she broke off as more footsteps were heard outside in the corridor – just one person's, light footed like a woman's.

For a moment they all froze, but then Miss Jardine swept in angrily and demanded to know why they had been taking so long.

"Mrs Ware-Gillow says she sent you up ages ago, Joanna; it's not as if I hadn't enough work to do without chasing after you children. Now go along *at once* and take the material with you. No, you can leave the pieces I'm working on." She went over to the sewing machine, sat down and proceeded to stitch away, turning the handle vigorously as if to show her irritation.

"Come and look at the picture, it's on the way down," Joanna whispered as they descended from the attic. They stared in silence at the portrait until Tony remarked "Nuns aren't usually young – you never see them looking like that."

"Yes, you do – we have one at the convent – Sister Annunciata looks just like that."

"That's a funny name. How do you like it at the convent?" Dip asked curiously.

"I hate it. You're so lucky being in your own homes and going to an ordinary school. The nuns are so strict and the girls are dreadful." It was good to be able to talk with someone her own age, "And I've got piles of homework to do; I bet you haven't any."

A vision of Cat's-eyes Cox passed fleetingly through Dip's mind and his fury over the last French exercise he'd handed in. He preferred not to think about homework.

39

"The only bright spot on the horizon is that my father may be coming on Tuesday," she said.

"Well, lucky you. We won't see our fathers until goodness knows when and Aunt Mabel is staying on as my father has a suspected appendicitis and is in hospital now, so Mother won't be home for ages and worst of all we're getting a lodger." Joanna looked taken aback by Dip's outburst. It was even more heated than her own.

In fact Dip had been grumbling to Tony all the way to the Hall that afternoon. Seemingly a Mr Arthur Finch had been planted on them by the Ministry of Agriculture. Apparently he was going to check up on the use of marsh grass as cattle fodder and was due to arrive the following morning.

"Aunt Mabel's grumbling like mad," he now explained to Joanna, "and she's afraid he's going to have an enormous appetite and the rations won't hold out."

Tony had heard all this already and was still studying the portrait. "She seems to be standing in a garden. – Is it this one, do you think?"

The other two looked at the portrait again with added interest. To the right of the figure was a small compact garden planted with box hedges which seemed to form some sort of pattern.

"It *is* this garden!" Joanna exclaimed. "I think it's what Mrs Ware-Gillow calls her 'Boxed h'in 'edge'. It's by the old stables. But it's not very well kept up nowadays." Joanna screwed her eyes up. "I think she must have had her portrait painted in an upstairs room with the window wide open because you can't see the pattern of the hedges from ground level."

Dip looked at his watch. "Come on – we'd better get going with this stuff. I've got to help Aunt Mabel get the boxroom ready for the new lodger."

Joanna was sorry to see them go. "Do you play tennis?" she asked. "Mrs Ware-Gillow said she'd get Moses to mark out the old grass-court sometime and I could ask a friend round to play." She didn't think Mrs Ware-Gillow had had two boys in mind when she'd suggested it, more likely what she described as "those beautifully be'aved young ladies from the Sacred 'Eart, some from very well connected families I 'ear."

Neither of the boys played tennis but Joanna persisted "Well, there's a good place to take Snipe the other side of the mere – if we can dodge Moses and his rabbit traps. We could take a picnic – Edwina would find some bits of food."

This sounded better and Dip said they'd come over one week-end. He added that Miss Linniment would be sending out a search party if they didn't turn up soon and they left, straining under the load of huge bundles of black fabric.

*　　*　　*

AT about half-past seven, Joanna presented herself in the drawing room. She had tried to tame her hair a little and brushed off some of the dust and cobwebs from the attic, which clung to her shapeless skirt.

"Oh Johanna – there you are – I was wondering what had kept you." Mrs Ware-Gillow's voice sounded plummy but she gave a cross smile. "May I present Johanna Palmer – Captain Palmer's daughter, you know. The Reverend and Miss Truce. You can come and sit down with us for a few minutes before we have dinner." This gracious offer was given in the manner of a great favour being bestowed.

The Reverend Aldous Truce was tall, thin, fair and angular but his smile was kindly and Miss Truce with her wispy hair could have been his twin. She was sitting on the sofa and patted one of the satin cushions. "Come and sit here." It was really the only available seat left, since Mr Ware-Gillow, had spread himself over the small two-seat sofa and looked liable to drop off to sleep any minute. The large black cat was getting ready to leave Mrs Ware-Gillow's lap any moment – it kept looking at the spare cushion with a contemplative stare. If there was one thing that made Miss Truce more nervous and jumpy than children (especially after the ordeal of those terrible evacuees) it was cats – she was almost allergic to them and Joanna seemed the lesser of the two evils.

"Ave you finished all your 'omework, Johanna?" Mrs Ware-Gillow asked, as she refilled the vicar's wine glass with a little more of her precious pre-war sherry.

"No, I've got to finish an essay on the Civil War and . . ."

"Ah – The Civil War," the vicar took an appreciative sip

41

of the sherry and sat back with his eyes half closed. "A most interesting period of our history – yes indeed. You know, of course, that much of the action took place in this area? Chester was under siege for two years – loyally supporting Charles I and you can see the tower on the City Walls from which he watched the Battle of Rowton Moor."

He paused for breath and took another sip of sherry.

"I've only just started learning about it at school – I don't think I'm much good at history. But," she remembered, "Edwina told me that the ghost who haunts this house was a nun who vanished during the Civil War and her lover was a Roundhead."

Mrs Ware-Gillow frowned furiously. "That's quite enough of that – the Reverend Truce doesn't wish to 'ear the ramblings of our parlour maid. Ghost indeed – the very idea!" She gave a short sarcastic laugh.

"Oh I don't know," the vicar smiled, "I'm very interested in local history – a little hobby of mine. I've heard vague stories of this nun but I didn't realise she originated from the Hall. I'd like to hear more about it some time – I'm writing a little paper on the history of the village, aren't I, Prudence?"

His sister nodded but kept a wary eye on Cleopatra who was stretching her legs and looked ready to spring at any moment.

"Up in one of the attics there's an old trunk full of papers and documents," Joanna went on helpfully. "I think they must have belonged to the people who used to live here."

"Is that so? – Most interesting, most interesting! Perhaps I may be allowed a little browse through them one afternoon with your permission?" He looked at Mrs Ware-Gillow who nodded rather curtly. The conversation was not going at all the way she'd planned – she knew nothing of history and had only agreed to come to live in this large dusty old house because 'hubby' had said it would suit their position in society, him being a Director of Huxley's Bakeries. She looked at her husband for a bit of support but he had dropped right off to sleep.

"Well, I think we'll go hin to dinner. Roast chicken," she added brightly, and rose rather stiffly, causing Cleopatra to jump down from her lap, Miss Truce to shrink back in fear and Mr Ware-Gillow to wake up with a snort.

Back in her room, Joanna sat by the window looking out at the garden in the dusk. It was peaceful and she could smell the scent of the wallflowers in the flower bed below. Her homework that evening was to write an essay on the causes of the Civil War. So far she had written half a page of dry facts gleaned from her text book – she had not really followed the lesson at school that morning which had seemed to consist of a number of dates and names quickly forgotten.

'The Civil War 1642–49 was a war which divided the country,' she reread, and then chewed the end of her pencil.

It must have been dreadful not knowing who to trust, she thought. 'There must have been spies like there are in this war . . . exactly 300 years ago. At least we're all united this time . . . I wonder who I would have supported – the King or Cromwell? Alice and her family supported the King . . . I wonder which was her bedroom? This one perhaps.'

She gazed out of the window again at the lengthening shadows and her day-dreaming stopped abruptly as a dark shadowy figure darted suddenly behind the elm trees and was gone before she'd had time to see it properly. What could it have been? The ghost of Alice Sayer? No, she had nuns on the brain. It was very probably just Cleopatra out for an evening's hunting. Joanna turned back to her essay.

CHAPTER FIVE

The man from the Ministry

ARTHUR FINCH soon made himself at home at Dean Farm. He was short, beady eyed and birdlike. He had been sent, he said, from the Ministry to find out if the marsh grass in this part of Cheshire could be used in the production of cattle food and he started his enquiries and investigations from the word go, putting a lot of people's backs up by poking around cottage gardens backing onto the marsh and peering into barns and pig-sties. He'd already been ticked off by Sylvia, the bad-tempered land-girl, before she realised who he was.

Aunt Mabel had taken charge of his ration-book and was juggling the amounts of food to the best of her ability. She had warned him, in case he had forgotten, that only 2 oz of tea, 2 oz of butter, 2 oz of cheese, 3 oz of margarine and one egg were allowed per person per week, had stressed that she couldn't work miracles and was very relieved that not only was he bird-like in appearance but in his appetite too. He tended to peck faddily at small amounts.

Having got that sorted out, she turned her attention to the pile of blackout material she was trying to turn into nuns' robes for the concert.

Miss Linniment had begged her to help and in a reckless moment she had promised not only to make some of the clothes but to act as prompter for a sketch based on the life of Florence Nightingale, written by one of the members.

She was not very handy with a needle and the sewing machine used by Dip's mother didn't seem to be working properly – the thread kept snapping as did Aunt Mabel's temper.

"A stitch in time, saves nine; patience is as patience does;

don't run before you can walk," Dip muttered under his breath, trying to find an appropriate saying for his aunt. She had persuaded him to act as a model for the garments and he was standing enveloped in black material when Arthur Finch came into the living room.

"Don't tell me, let me guess," he stood in the doorway with his hands pressed together. "I know – the three witches of Macbeth, rolled into one, – no – a black pudding," he beamed at his own cleverness.

Peter laughed, "Yes, a black pudding."

Dip scowled. He was wondering when things would get back to normal. He longed for Mum and Dad to be there. He thought of the four of them having supper together, alone. Instead of which Aunt Mabel seemed to be staying for ever, and he was covered in smelly hot black fabric with a complete stranger making fun of him. He tolerated Mr Finch but he hadn't really taken to him. He and Tony had nicknamed him Chiffchaff and had made him into a bit of a joke figure – that way it wasn't quite so bad having him around the place.

Peter had taken to him right away – perhaps because Arthur Finch didn't eat sweets. He had arrived with several weeks' rations, bought in London, and had promptly given the whole lot to Peter, who now followed him round, no doubt hoping for more where those had come from. It made Dip feel sick.

"I think that will do, dear," Aunt Mabel sighed. The costumes didn't look right. They hung badly and were rather skimpy but, 'it will be all right on the night,' she kept telling herself, hopefully.

"We are having the dress rehearsal in ten days. Miss Linnament was rather hoping that you and some of the other young people in the village might contribute in some way. A recitation perhaps – you could do 'The Wreck of The Hesperus', something in that line or maybe a nice little song about the spring . . .?" She trailed off doubtfully, catching sight of Dip's fiercely defensive expression.

Arthur Finch cleared his throat, "I was wondering if young David here would escort me to Shottington Hall this evening? I have to make one or two enquiries there – I believe part of their property runs down to the marsh. We could set out directly after . . . er, tea, perhaps."

45

"Oh – it's quite easy to find," Dip said. "Just go straight down the lane and . . ."

"Of *course* you'll do as Mr Finch asks, David – I won't hear another word about it," Aunt Mabel said sternly.

"I'll come too," Peter gave a winning smile.

"Indeed you'll do no such thing – had you forgotten I promised to finish *With Rod and Gun* this evening?"

"Tony's coming round; we were going to give Snipe some training," Dip objected.

"You can both go to the Hall together then, with Mr Finch." Aunt Mabel brought the subject to a close by sweeping out of the room to prepare the sausage and mash.

Dip decided it wouldn't be so bad if Tony came too. They could soon lose Chiffchaff at the Hall and Joanna might be in the garden. Perhaps Edwina would give them some ginger biscuits and maybe they could have another look at the air-raid shelter in the rockery – it had fascinated him – the sheer luxury of it, hidden away like that.

Tony arrived after tea and together with Arthur Finch and Snipe, bounding along happily, they walked along Shottington Lane. Everything seemed to be bursting into flower. The hawthorn was in blossom and Queen Anne's lace and pink campion lined the way.

Eric Bulley passed them on his way to a Home Guard meeting at the village hall and a bus, going to Chester an hour late, rattled along rapidly, making the grasses in the hedgerow shake in the wind as it passed.

"Have you heard Miss Linniment wants us to do a number in the concert?" Dip eyed Tony mischievously. "A duet or something, she said, or an Ivor Novello number or a Vera Lynn song. Something sentimental that really touches them here." He put his hand to his heart and rolled his eyes.

"Well, she'll have to think again, won't she?" Tony growled. "Mind you," he added, brightening a bit, "we *could* put on quite a good exhibition with our shrapnel collection and ask people to guess where we found different pieces or what sort of bomb they came off." He warmed to the theme. "I bet they'd like that better than a lot of old women singing and acting. *Or* I could do my impersonations of Spitfires and Lancasters."

46

The two fell silent, contemplating this idea of livening up the show.

Arthur Finch, who had been lost in his own thoughts for a while, suddenly said, "What do you know of the Ware-Gillows, boys? You've lived in this area a good while. How long have they been here?"

"About two or three years I think," Dip replied as he led the way along the main drive to the Hall. "Look, there's Moses!" He turned to Tony and pointed to a figure in brown dungarees tending a bonfire in the distance. Snipe barked as a wood pigeon fluttered out of a tree and the figure by the fire straightened up.

"He's the chauffeur, game-keeper, gardener and odd job man. He's just the person you want to talk to – as long as you can speak Welsh!"

Dip and Tony watched for a moment while Mr Finch stepped out jauntily to interrogate the surly-looking Moses and then darted away in the opposite direction.

There was a strange car standing beside the house, but no sign of Joanna. "Let's go and have another look at their 'dug-out'," Dip said, "Come on." They found their way to the rockery, opened the wooden door and remembered to look for the torch on the shelf. They followed the steps to the inner door and through it to the shelter. Tony lit the oil lamp and Dip stretched himself out on a leopard-skin rug on one of the bunk beds and picked up an old copy of *The Tatler*. "This is the life!" he sighed.

A minute or two later they were horrified to hear the unmistakable sounds of someone approaching. The outer door banged open.

"Oh no!" Dip whispered hoarsely.

"I can't find the torch," someone said.

"Ah, so this is where you go when there's an air raid," replied a man's voice. "Now I'll be able to imagine you safely tucked in when the sirens go."

The thick inner door creaked open and there was Joanna with the tall figure of a man, who stooped as he came through the doorway carrying a lighted match. The two looked surprised to see the boys reclining on the bunk beds. They jumped up rather shame-facedly and tried to think of some good excuse, but Joanna was pleased to see them. "These are my friends, Dip and Tony – this is my father."

"Had a heavy day at work, I suppose," Captain Palmer said smiling. He had the same bright blue eyes as Joanna and they crinkled when he smiled. Perhaps they looked even bluer than they were because of his tanned face. Although he had left the sea for his shore posting in Liverpool he carried a distinctly nautical air about him.

"We came over with Chiffchaff – that's to say Mr Finch. He's the man from the Ministry of Agriculture and goes round inspecting the land to see if they can make cattle food from the marsh grass; I think that's what he does anyway," Tony explained.

"Finch, eh?" Captain Palmer looked as if he was going to say something else but changed his mind. "This is the height of luxury, isn't it?" He commented looking round.

"How about a cup of coffee?" Joanna asked.

"Well, that sounds like a very good idea," her father said.

Dip lit the primus and filled the kettle with water from a large container which had a little tap in the side and Joanna found the bottle of Camp coffee, and four cups. "They're china, so we'll have to be careful. Mrs Ware-Gillow doesn't like roughing it."

"This brings back memories." Captain Palmer put a spoonful of dried milk into the cup of coffee and sniffed it. "We used to drink this stuff in Malta – we had crates of it."

"My father's in the Navy – he's been to Malta too." Dip seized at the link with his father – it made him seem a little nearer for a minute. As they drank their coffee the Captain talked to them about the Navy and about Dunkirk where he had been wounded. It was following his time in hospital that he had been sent to Liverpool.

"I can't tell you anything about my present job of course, except that it is vital for the life blood of this country that our ships get through from America. The enemy is well aware of our dependence on them, of course, and they will do all in their power to break through our security to discover when and where our convoys are sailing. Too many boats are being torpedoed. It begins to look as though there is a serious leakage of information." His eyes had taken on a far-away, worried look. "Something more than a chain of coincidences . . ."

"Do you mean . . . spies?" Dip asked.

"Perhaps – something of the sort," Joanna's father smiled absently. "But remember – it's up to us all to keep our eyes and ears open at all times. You never know when any scrap of information, however small, may come in useful – vitally useful. Danger can be all around us, in our everyday lives, living among us, unrecognised." He went on to tell them about a spy who had lived in Portsmouth in the last war and had passed himself off as a doctor. "He was very popular with his patients."

"Gosh," Dip said, wondering about their village G.P.

"I'd better take these cups back and wash them, before Mrs Ware-Gillow notices they've been used," Joanna said and her father rose to his feet.

"Good girl," he said. "And talking of Mrs Ware-Gillow, I promised her I'd look in for a sherry before starting back for Liverpool."

"Oh, Daddy, – you don't have to go yet, do you?"

"I'm afraid so, in about half an hour, but we've got our day in Chester to look forward to, haven't we? You can bring a friend or two with you, if you like," he added quietly as the two boys went ahead with the torch. "We can have a picnic at the zoo – I hear it's a very good one, and perhaps there'll be a good film to see afterwards."

"I'll ask Dip and Tony, not any of the girls from school – especially not Francesca Stewart – she's dreadful," Joanna told him. But a week on Saturday seemed like a year away.

Snipe had been very patient in the shelter but decided he had earned a little exercise now and Tony had to run to keep up with him. Over a box hedge, in a part of the garden the boys hadn't seen before, they saw a familiar figure – Mr Finch waving his arms as if he was describing the width of a trench.

"He looks as if he's about to take flight," Tony laughed. Moses Jones appeared to be glowering at whatever Arthur Finch was demonstrating.

"That's the knot garden," said Joanna joining them. They looked over the hedge, which was about waist-level, and saw a pattern of hedges and paths. "It's very old and all the plants inside the design are herbs – things like mint and sage. It's really meant to be seen from an upstairs room and then you can see the pattern properly – that's what my father said. In the past, most large country houses had one and they used the herbs as medicine and to disguise the taste of bad food sometimes."

"We could do with one at school," Dip muttered.

"I must remember to look for a room which overlooks this part of the garden next time I'm upstairs."

Arthur Finch looked as if he was still engrossed in his conversation so Joanna suggested they go and see if Edwina had any ginger biscuits, while her father was having his sherry. She tentatively suggested the expedition to Chester and was pleased when Dip and Tony were enthusiastic about the idea.

In the kitchen, Edwina found not only ginger biscuits but some of Cook's special carrot cake left over from tea.

They all laughed when Joanna told them about the 'ghost' she'd seen from the window the other night.

"No more ghost stories for you, my girl; I'll be accused of putting strange fancies into your head," Edwina said grimly.

Arthur Finch popped his head round the door and was persuaded to peck at a ginger biscuit.

They decided to take Mr Finch back to Barton by the marsh path. The estuary had once been busy with ships going up the river as far as Chester, but had started silting up in the seventeenth century and the water had now receded as far as Portgate. Grass had taken over, providing good pasture for sheep and cattle and was a favourite haunt of wild fowl that nested in the reeds by the pools and channels left by the receding tide. In the spring and autumn high tides sometimes covered the marshes as far up as Barton but at the moment with the weather dry and sunny, the marsh looked like one enormous pasture, concealing its treacherous gulleys and quicksands.

"I'm a bit of a bird fancier myself," Arthur Finch confided as they walked along. "I must bring my field-glasses down here sometime – this is a first class place to do a spot of watching."

Snipe was ambling along contentedly and Tony was relieved to see he took no interest in the grazing sheep. He found a dead seagull festering beside a stagnant pool and paused to investigate it.

Two nuns from the convent school taking an evening stroll looked at Snipe and his prey with distaste and averted their eyes.

"Leave it alone, there's a good boy." Tony clipped the lead on to Snipe's collar and pulled and tugged until he reluctantly left the exciting smell.

"Look, isn't that a reed warbler?" Arthur Finch screwed up his eyes and peered out towards the Welsh hills. "And there go some shellduck!" he cried excitedly.

"What have you got now?" Dip bent down and took something out of Snipe's mouth.

"It's a chocolate wrapper – I suppose it still has the smell of chocolate on it."

"Poor old Snipe – nothing to eat there."

"Mmm, chocolate – I haven't tasted any for ages – I had a boiled sweet last week," Tony reminisced. "What sort was it – milk or plain – I wonder what lucky person managed to get their hands on that?"

Dip straightened out the scrap of paper – "I don't know – it looks like foreign writing . . . Julius Meinl," he read out slowly, "Choc something . . . Gottingen . . . I can't read the rest, it's faded."

"We mustn't leave litter lying around the marshes, must we?" Mr Finch held out his hand for the wrapper and popped it swiftly into his pocket.

CHAPTER SIX

Sanctuary

DIP decided to look up 'Gottingen' when he got home. It sounded foreign but his atlas was an old school one and not very comprehensive and it yielded no clue.

There was a much better selection of maps and atlases in Tony's house, because his father was a geography master – so after tea the next afternoon the two boys pored over a pile of them on the kitchen table.

"Any luck?" Dip asked after a while.

"No – nothing – and I don't know where to begin looking."

"What are you two doing – you look very studious?" Tony's grandfather came through to prepare a bran mash for the hens.

"We're looking for a place called 'Gottingen', but I think we'll have to give up."

It had been raining all day but had now stopped and was turning out to be a nice evening. "Let's give it up and take Snipe for some exercise before it gets dark – he's been cooped up all day – I'll fetch his lead," Tony said.

Snipe went mad with excitement when he heard the rattle of the lead – barking and jumping up at the boys.

"What was that name again?" Grandpa shouted above the din. "I seem to remember there's a European Atlas with a very good index that your dad kept on the top shelf in the sitting-room. If I have a moment I'll have a look for you."

"*Gottingen*", Tony shouted back, before he was pulled out through the door by Snipe.

They decided to go up into the woods. It was cool and dark and the trees were still dripping after the downpour. There was a smell of wet earth and pine needles and the ground felt squelchy.

"We'd better not go too near 'Mad Kate's'; someone said she had nineteen cats at the last count," Dip warned. "If Snipe got among that lot . . ." They could see her small, picturesque but dilapidated cottage in the distance, with smoke rising from a chimney pot perched precariously on the stack. The windows were tiny and the roof needed rethatching; changing architectural fashions had passed it by since the time it had been built in the seventeenth century.

"Do you think she really *is* mad?" Tony asked. The two of them had discussed this often enough with relish but never came up with a satisfactory answer. Children would run when they saw her coming. Kate Murphy was certainly eccentric, wandering round the village and woods at all hours, dressed

in a collection of dark flowing clothes and shawls, muttering to herself. Her family had come over from Ireland during the potato famine and had scratched a living in Barton – doing odd jobs – helping on farms, gardening, making wooden clothes pegs and rag rugs. Then at the turn of the century a plague of typhoid in the village had wiped out the few remaining members of her family who hadn't gone to seek their fortune further afield – leaving only Kate alone in the cottage. She had escaped the typhoid but had become increasingly withdrawn over the years – collecting stray cats – a wild, thin bunch which hunted mice and small birds in the woods. No one knew Kate's exact age – she looked a perpetual seventy but could have been younger or a great deal older. She lived a fiercely independent life – growing a few potatoes on a patch of land at the back of the cottage and drawing water from an ancient well; and she was the bane of Miss Linniment's life. She would like to see her settled in a neat new council house or looked after properly in the local almshouses. At the very least she wanted to clear out all those smelly cats, fumigate the cottage and have a proper water system installed. But Kate was having none of it and Miss Linniment had almost given up trying, except to say wistfully every so often "Something *must* be done about Kate Murphy!"

"There goes one of her cats now." Dip spied a mangey tabby bounding through the trees – it looked very different to the sleek confident Celopatra. "Gone to look for some supper I suppose, – hold on to Snipe – I think he's spotted her!"

But he was too late; Snipe had already dashed off in pursuit and was almost at once side-tracked by an interesting scent close to a large rabbit hole, and in an instant he had disappeared down it. The boys could hear muffled barkings coming up from the warren and wondered what was going on in the earth below.

It should have been still quite light with 'double summertime' in force. Because of the war, clocks had been put forward two hours to give extra daylight working hours for farmers. However, this evening it was overcast and sultry. Cheerfully at first, but then with increasing anxiety, the boys waited and whistled. After a time a spot of rain fell and it looked as if there would be a good deal more any minute.

"What on earth are we going to do?" Tony peered down the

54

rabbit hole again as Snipe showed no signs of reappearing.

"D'you think he's got stuck down there?" Dip said anxiously. The thought of the dog being trapped was alarming – it would be like lying in the cellar during an air-raid wondering if you'd be buried under the rubble of the house. "We must try to get him out."

They called him again and again but there was no sound now except the steady fall of rain on the leaves overhead. Suddenly there came a noise that was only too familiar – the slow crescendo of the siren rising and falling with persistent wailing over the surrounding countryside, sending everyone scattering to shelter.

"It's early, isn't it?" Dip shouted in a hoarse voice. "We don't usually get raids while it's light."

"Never mind that," Tony shouted back. "What are we going to do about Snipe?" He started banging frantically over the hole with his fists.

"Don't do that – you'll cause an avalanche inside!"

It was raining heavily now; the wail of the siren had died away. Very faintly from a long way away, they heard the unmistakable droning of an aeroplane.

The looked at each other desperately. At that moment a scuffling sound from down in the ground, reached their ears. Tony shouted down the hole "Here boy!" and in a few seconds Snipe appeared, shuffling backwards, covered in soil and twigs, unaware of the worry he'd caused. They grabbed hold of him and started to run, half stumbling, down through the woods.

The plane sounded nearer. "Let's shelter in the church," Dip shouted, gasping for breath. "We can go down into the crypt."

The massive form of the tower loomed up in front of them, as they raced down the three sandstone steps, and along the path through the graveyard to the studded door of the porch. It looked invincible. Dip turned the iron ring handle and the door opened up.

Inside the air struck chill, but the solid sandstone walls seemed safe and protective. Over the porch, the tower rose to a height of 110 feet, the highest point in the village. On a clear day it commanded wonderful views. There was a small stout door which opened onto narrow steep sandstone steps leading in a spiral to the very top of the tower. It was at present unsafe, because of a recent landmine, and no one was supposed to go up it.

Dip wedged Snipe's lead under one of the large Norman stones, part of all that remained of the original twelfth century church, before entering the main part of the church. The door which led down to the crypt was at the back of the nave. As the boys quietly pushed open the door, which was already ajar, from the porch into the church, the air had a slightly musty smell of old kneelers and hymn books, despite one of Miss Truce's flower arrangements on the altar of pansies, wallflowers, blue bells and cow parsley.

But there was something else; a feeling that they were not alone in the church although the shodowy pews were uninhabited and there was no one in the pulpit. In the dim light, the choir stalls appeared to be empty, but Dip suddenly felt his blood run cold as, over by the organ, a dark shadow rose up. He gripped Tony's arm and the two watched in horrified fascination the slow gliding movements of a figure dressed all in black, as it approached the organ. It seemed to have no face but a bony white hand stretched out, reaching for the organ keys. Then above the sound of the rain lashing against the windows and the wind blowing the swaying branches of the yew trees, they heard something else – a series of notes being picked out, not a proper tune – high pitched and discordant. The music had an unearthly, eerie quality, without a proper beginning or end. It finished on a note which sounded all wrong, even to Dip's unmusical ear, but it was a haunting sequence of notes, repeated again

and again. He tugged Tony's sleeve with an icy, shaking hand and nodded towards the half open crypt door. Stealthily, on hands and knees they crept towards it and once through, Dip pulled it to behind them. The door was old and heavy and creaked with what sounded to them like a deafening noise. Terrified, they held their breath but didn't dare peer round towards the choir stalls.

Then they sensed rather than heard the soft padded footsteps coming slowly down the aisle and pausing by the entrance to the crypt. Dip thought he was going to faint, but to his great relief the steps continued again out into the porch.

"Snipe!" Tony's face was deathly white as he mouthed the word, but almost immediately another door was opened and from overhead came the muffled sound of someone climbing the bell tower. "Let's get out while we've got the chance," Dip hissed. As silently as they could, they crept out into the porch where, to their relief, they found Snipe fast asleep behind the Norman stones. Quickly Tony pulled the lead free and they ran out of the church, not stopping until they reached Dean Farm where they banged on the door until it was flung open by Aunt Mabel.

"What in the world are you two doing?" She dragged them in quickly. "Don't you know there's a raid on? I thought you were both at Tony's house." She looked at them accusingly. Water dripped off their soaked clothes as they followed her, white and shaken, down into the cellar.

"We were caught in the woods," Dip started to explain.

"We lost Snipe and it started to rain," Tony added. "Then we heard the siren and sheltered in the church but we, we . . ." he didn't know how to go on. "We heard some strange noises and there was a figure all in black and . . ."

But Aunt Mabel, who was only half listening, was eyeing the puddles at their feet. "I never heard such nonsense," she said briskly. "You should have stayed *put* – better safe than sorry! No, don't sit on the blankets, you'll make them all wet; sit over there on the bench. You're very lucky I heard you at the door, I was keeping one ear open for Mr Finch; gracious knows where he's got to." She picked up some navy blue knitting and turned to Peter who had made himself comfortable on a pile of blankets and old cushions. "Now, where had we got to?'' She found her place in a copy of *Play Up, St Monica's* and read aloud: ''Norah O'Brien had just been made Captain of Hockey and Madge Patterson was going to spill the beans about the apple pie bed . . .''

There was no opportunity for further discussion about the frightening figure in the church and the boys had to listen, still feeling shaken, to the tale of rivalry, jealousies and triumphs at St Monica's, as Aunt Mabel read on relentlessly until the All Clear sounded.

''Well, we'll have to leave it there for the moment.'' Aunt Mabel sounded reluctant as she closed the book and pushed her knitting away into a linen bag bulging with odds and ends of wool and knitting patterns.

The boys got up thankfully and Snipe shook himself all over everyone, covering them in showers of wet and mud. Aunt Mabel opened her mouth to make an angry remark but at that minute there was some more banging at the back door and she and Peter went up to see who was there.

''Tony, what do you think it was up at the church? Was it a ghost?'' Dip was bursting to talk about what they'd seen, as soon as the other two were out of earshot.

''I don't know,'' Tony said thoughtfully. ''I suppose it could be – it looked like – I know it sounds silly – but it looked like a nun.''

''Perhaps the church is haunted as well as the Hall. Perhaps that piece of music she plays is a sort of lament – a sort of warning or something,'' Dip warmed to his theme. ''Maybe it's only heard every hundred years or so, when there's danger lurking about!''

''I don't know – perhaps there's a more simple explanation – someone just practising or tuning the keys. Grandpa heard something like it the other evening – don't you remember, I told you?''

''Yes, but he didn't see what *we* saw,'' Dip insisted. ''Should we tell anyone, do you think?''

''Who'd believe us if we said it was a ghostlike figure? Although, I suppose Grandpa might be interested.''

''In what?'' asked a familiar voice. Stooping as he came slowly down the steps, Tony's grandfather looked at the two boys with relief. ''I was sure you'd have the sense to run here

58

when the air raid warning went. Funny time of day, wasn't it? Must have been a lone German plane lost after a raid. Probably trying to find its way home again, chased by some of our lads. You boys look soaking wet – you'd better come home now, Tony, and get into some dry clothes.''

"We sheltered in the church but there was someone there – a figure all in black, and some weird music like this.'' Dip whistled, giving a fair imitation of the notes they'd heard. "Didn't you hear someone at the organ the other evening?''

Grandpa laughed. ''Yes, I did hear something but I don't think it was very significant – just someone picking out a few notes while waiting there for the vicar or the verger, I imagine.''

"But the person we saw was dressed all in black robes – over her head, you know – like a nun.''

"You probably saw old Kate sheltering from the rain – with a black shawl over her head – perhaps she was trying to pick out a few notes of an old Irish lullaby! Come on now, Tony, your mother's cooking a rabbit pie this evening and I'm ready for it.'' He was impatient to be off, and they followed him out of the cellar.

"I expect he's right,'' Tony turned to say to Dip. He was beginning to feel a bit sheepish at the way they'd panicked.

"By the way, I looked up that place you wanted – Gottingen – and found it in one of your father's old atlases. In Germany it was – still is probably.''

"Thanks,'' Dip said, but his mind was still taken up by the fright they'd had in the church.

*   *   *

ARTHUR FINCH returned at about eight o'clock.

"I was down at one of those barley fields by the marsh and had to take refuge in a disused sheep shelter.'' He looked put out and his indignation clearly increased while after a sparse supper of cold corned beef hash he had to listen with Peter to another stirring episode of *Play Up St Monica's*.

CHAPTER SEVEN

A scrap of silk

"FORTY – love;" the clear, rather arrogant tones of Francesca Stewart rang across the tennis lawn at the Hall. The lawn had been mown, rolled and marked by Moses Jones, grumbling and complaining incomprehensibly while he did it.

Mrs Ware-Gillow had been pleased with the result and without consulting Joanna, had rung up the convent and suggested Francesca should come over at the week-end and play tennis. She decided they would take tea in the summerhouse afterwards, with cucumber sandwiches and chocolate cake. She'd have to have a word with Cook. One might as well do the thing properly. She'd made rather a good chocolate cake herself once, in the days before she had a cook – with a rich filling and delicious sticky icing. She sighed – how she and Joe had enjoyed it. No one seemed to be able to make a proper cake these days. Of course with all the rationing it wasn't possible. The very thought of it filled her with hunger. She wondered if she should have the lawn in front of the house mown very closely and the old croquet hoops set out just to give the finishing touch to the perfect English scene, but she lost her nerve at the sight of Moses' face, black as thunder as he pushed the heavy rollers across the tennis lawn. It was no good antagonising the man – 'Goodness knows' she told herself, 'he's far from perfect but if he walks out what on earth will we do?' She was pleased that Francesca Stewart, or Francesca McNab Stewart to give her her proper name, had accepted the invitation. It was gratifying to entertain the daughter of the famous Edinburgh architect F. McNab Stewart – everyone had heard of him – he was sure to get a knighthood one of these days. She'd looked him up in Josiah's *Who's Who* so that she could talk knowledgeably to his daughter about the buildings he'd designed.

Joanna was cross with herself for ever mentioning the girl's name to Mrs Ware-Gillow. Of all the pupils at the Sacred Heart, Francesca was probably the one she liked least. Supercilious, self confident, good at games and very attractive, she either ignored Joanna or talked about her in whispers and with sidelong glances, to her friends. Joanna hadn't been able to understand why Francesca had decided to come and play tennis with her until she overheard her discuss it with another girl. "I know it's a terrible bore, but the Hall is very old so my father will be fascinated to hear all about it. I only hope I'll have an opportunity to look round. Anyway it's a day out and anything's better than being stuck in school on Saturday."

For Joanna the only bright spot in the afternoon was that Dip and Tony had surprisingly turned up just before Francesca.

*　　　*　　　*

MISS LINNIMENT was in one of her 'states'. One of the nun's habits for the concert was missing. "Either that, or we underestimated the amount of material needed," she said. Four people in the village, including herself, had been busy sewing the robes and now somehow they were one short and no one could remember the exact number each had promised to make. Aunt Mabel had taken it personally when Miss Linniment called round, fussing and worried.

"Does she think I've kept one back? She practically accused me of stealing one of them," she stormed indignantly at Dip. "Out of the kindness of my heart I offered to help and I did my best, I'm sure, and that's all the thanks I get." She paused, searching in her mind for an apt proverb which would do justice to the situation but none sprang to mind.

"She doesn't really think you've hidden one," Dip tried to pacify his aunt. "She's just got muddled – Miss Jardine at the Hall may have some more material – Tony and I will go over to see."

*　　　*　　　*

WHEN the boys arrived at the Hall, Miss Jardine bustled off angrily, muttering that she supposed she'd have to go and look in the attics as if she hadn't got enough to do, and why couldn't Miss Linniment keep a more careful check on things? She was quite sure she'd given her enough material for ten costumes. Her voice grew fainter as she climbed the stairs, leaving the boys in the cool hall where Joanna found them and eventually persuaded them to stay and play tennis with the dreaded Francesca.

Mrs Ware-Gillow swept by. "Now don't forget to come and find me when your little friend arrives; I'm looking forward to meeting her. What are you two boys doing 'ere?" Her voice sharpened abruptly as she saw Dip and Tony from under the brim of her enormous straw sun hat.

"They came to collect some more black material and I've asked them to play tennis. It's better with four. We can play doubles," Joanna said rather defiantly.

"Oh, very well, although I don't know what the Mother Superior will say, I'm sure." It was too hot to argue, and it suited her mood to be gracious this afternoon. She had got Moses Jones to put a deckchair and cushions in a shady spot by the knot garden where she could have a little rest. She had the daughter of an eminent architect coming to tea – the boys would surely be gone by then – and cook had made a very passable chocolate cake.

Francesca had been accompanied by Sister Annunciata – a tall young nun with a pale oval face and large dark eyes. Her voice was low with a pronounced foreign accent.

Seeing her all in black with white wimple reminded Dip of the figure he'd seen in the church and he shivered slightly when she turned towards him. She smiled slightly as he was introduced and at once he thought of the portrait upstairs – she looked so like the young woman in the painting. 'I suppose *all* nuns look alike in those black clothes,' he told himself.

When she had gone, Joanna said "It must be dreadful for her, being trapped in England – perhaps she'll never be able to get back to Austria." She understood a little of what Sister Annunciata must have felt – being in a strange place with no immediate prospect of going back home, but Francesca standing there tall and immaculate in her tennis whites said sneeringly "If you ask me, she's probably a spy – look at all those letters she writes and the way she prowls around on her own.''

"I expect she's homesick," Joanna said quickly.

"Oh, you're just defending her because she talks to you sometimes. I expect she feels sorry for you," Francesca said with a touch of scorn. Joanna flushed. "Where's the tennis court?" She swung her racquet impatiently as if practising a forehand drive. "I didn't come here to discuss the nuns – glad to see the back of them for an afternoon." She raised an eyebrow and glanced about her appreciatively, her blue eyes taking in the oak staircase, the carved balustrades and wooden corbels. It *had* been worth coming, after all. The house was a gem – Tudor with later additions, she decided – and couldn't wait to explore, preferably on her own.

The tennis game was a fiasco. The boys determined to play together. Neither had played before – cricket was their summer game and the ancient racquets with missing strings, which had been found for them in the cloakroom, didn't help matters. They missed shot after shot and started to dissolve into helpless laughter, making exaggerated sweeps at the ball, which made Francesca, who took her game seriously, furious. She rounded

on Joanna: "I didn't expect to be playing with two idiots!"

Dip lunged viciously at the next ball and it sailed up into the sky and vanished in a pile of undergrowth in the direction of the mere.

"*Now* look what you've done," Francesca stormed and threw her racquet down in a rage.

"Let's go and look for it," Dip shouted and he, Tony and Joanna ran off, beating down nettles with their racquets and leaving Francesca scowling, on the court. The sun beat down remorselessly. "Let's go down to the mere" Dip suggested. "It'll be nice and cool down there and we can leave *her* to play by herself."

The search for the tennis ball was abandoned. "We can't just *leave* her there." Joanna wanted to escape just as much as the boys but knew she would pay for it at school next week. They glanced back through the undergrowth and saw Mrs Ware-Gillow appear, waddling round the corner of the house, her sun hat quivering at every step. She'd had a nice little doze in the knot garden and thought she would look in on the tennis match. The others lay low; they couldn't hear exactly what was said but to their relief saw the two go off together, Francesca doing the talking and Mrs Ware-Gillow looking flattered and pleased. As soon as they were out of sight, Joanna and the boys raced down to the mere, where there was a small wooden jetty at which a punt had once been tied up. They took off their shoes, and sitting on the jetty dangled their feet in the cool water, while the leaves from the oak and beech trees overhead gave them some welcome shelter.

"Phew – this is better than rotten old tennis." Dip slashed his feet, startling some mallard ducks which were resting in the water under the overhanging rhododendrons.

"And that girl . . ." words failed Tony.

"*I* didn't want her to come," Joanna protested, "but I wish Sister Annunciata could have stayed – she's really nice and she seems so lonely. She came over from Austria just before the war and can't get back again: she's stuck here, maybe forever."

"Yes – war divides people doesn't it?" Dip lay back, screwing up his eyes to look at the cool branches above. "There must be thousands of ordinary people like us in Germany and Austria and Italy who don't want to fight but have to do what their leaders say – not *everyone's* bad because they're Germans.''

"It must have been worse during the English Civil War when there wasn't even any real enemy. Families turned against each other and old friends; you wouldn't know who to trust – like Alice Sayer, the nun in the picture upstairs, torn between her family and her lover,'' Joanna said dramatically.

"Talking of nuns" – Dip made a sudden decision to tell Joanna of their experience in the church the other evening. While Tony skimmed pebbles across the mere he told her about the figure dressed in black and the eerie music, and watched her reaction. She didn't laugh or say he was imagining things. She accepted it seriously.

"I think I'd have been too frightened to run away – do you really think it was a ghost? I thought it was *this* house that was meant to be haunted – in fact I told you that I thought *I* saw a dark figure flit across the lawn when I was looking out of my window. Though I suppose it could have been the cat, Cleopatra,'' she added truthfully.

Tony turned round and looked sceptical. "Of course it was just the cat and what *we* saw was old Kate, like Grandad said.''

Dip shrugged his shoulders and made a face – the odd times he'd glimpsed Kate calling her cats up in the woods, she'd worn a ragged shawl which didn't cover her wild, straggling locks. He had never seen her completely shrouded in black. Still, it was too hot to argue. He turned his gaze upward again and his eye was at once caught by something pale, fluttering high among the branches of the tree; a butterfly perhaps, or one of Mrs Ware-Gillow's handkerchiefs. No, it was too small to be a hanky. It tantalised him: although it was out of reach it seemed to beckon him. What was it doing up there in the oak tree? Where had it blown from?

"I'm going to see what that scrap is up there." He pointed to the branch of the oak tree and the others followed his gaze.

"What, that rag? It's nothing; you're crazy. That branch wouldn't support your weight," Tony mocked.

"Well, we'll see." Tony's dismissive words made Dip more determined to climb the tree. The lower branches were large and accommodating and he managed them easily, but footrests were more difficult to find the higher he climbed. He lost his

sense of direction and had to shout to the others down below to point to the right branch. He negotiated it at last and slowly and painfully, inch by inch, crawled along it while it creaked under his weight. Smaller branches and twigs poked him in the ear and eye and caught at his hair. He could just make out the pale scrap, almost hidden by leaves – not too far away now – just another couple of feet. He pulled himself along a little further and felt the bough bending. It was almost within his grasp; he reached out and his hand closed over it.

At the same moment there was an ominous crack. "Look out!" Tony shouted. The branch, old and brittle, snapped and crashed down into the water below, hurtling Dip in with a loud splash. He surfaced almost immediately, his hand still clenched, and grinned triumphantly at the others who were peering anxiously into the water.

"Well, I hope it was worth it," Tony muttered as he took Dip's other hand and yanked him up out of the mud and weeds. "You smell awful!"

From behind a stout beech tree nearby, a figure emerged carrying a pair of field glasses. "What are you up to, you children?" a thin reed-like voice called.

"It's old Chiffchaff," Tony hissed to Dip.

"Just cooling off, Mr Finch," Dip shouted. "He seems to get everywhere," he added in a quieter voice to Tony and Joanna.

"Oh, it's you David; – whatever is your aunt going to say when she sees the mess you're in – and what are you doing here anyway? These are private grounds you know." He came towards them, samples of grasses sticking out of his pocket.

"I live here," Joanna said indignantly.

"We've been collecting some material and playing tennis and we're having tea with Mrs Ware-Gillow. What are *you* doing, Mr Finch?" Dip's fingers closed on the piece of fabric in his pocket – drenched like the rest of him.

"I've been reconnoitering the area – there's a terrible waste of acreage at the moment – it seems to me a duck farm would go nicely over there." He waved a hand vaguely. "Very nutritious, duck eggs – and talking of duck – did you spot those mallards?"

Despite the heat, Dip was beginning to shiver. "You'd better come in and get into something dry, though I can't think what!" Joanna said. They made their way back to the Hall, Dip's shoes squelching and squeaking, without meeting anyone else.

In the kitchen Edwina was organising tea, balancing tea-cups on the tray with a plate of sandwiches and a large chocolate cake.

"Good heavens, whatever have *you* been up to?" She put her finger and thumb delicately over her nose, saying "Keep away from my tray!" But she good naturedly found a towel and told Dip to go and clean himself up in the cloakroom and then hurriedly went to find an old woollen sweater of her own and a dressing-gown which had seen better days. Tony spread Dip's shirt and shorts on a bush to dry out in the sun.

Arthur Finch had somehow attached himself to the group and they made an odd procession as they went to find Francesca and Mrs Ware-Gillow in the summer house. Dip led the way, his hair standing on end in half dried tufts, the dressing-gown trailing on the ground.

They found the other two discussing the finer points of architecture. Francesca was airing her views on the Italian Renaissance – and Mrs Ware-Gillow was agreeing with every point. They broke off in mid sentence as the rest of the tea party appeared.

This was not at all the scene Mrs Ware-Gillow had imagined,

in which she would be pouring tea for two genteel girls, holding elegant conversation and discreetly nibbling sandwiches and cake. Why was that boy dressed like an oriental? Why was the other one smeared with mud? What was that tiresome man Arthur Finch doing here again? She sighed and asked Edwina to bring an extra cup and saucer. It was the war – nothing was the same – still, she supposed, she must do her bit.

"Francesca was saying that the pargeting on the wall 'ere is rare in this part of the country, weren't you dear?" She passed round the paste sandwiches.

The chocolate cake was delicious and Mrs Ware-Gillow was dismayed to see it disappearing fast. She'd hoped it would last for two or three days – she and Joe liked a piece of cake with their tea every afternoon.

Moses had been lighting one of his interminable bonfires and the smoke drifted over the tea party. Francesca coughed.

"It really is *too* bad," Mrs Ware-Gillow complained. "I'm going to speak to 'im about it – I think he does it on purpose. 'E'll burn the knot garden down if he's not careful – everything's as dry as dust in this 'eat." She brushed the crumbs from her lap and went to find Moses.

"That knot garden would make a marvellous place for vegetables," Arthur Finch murmured, and pecked at a ginger biscuit.

"Oh, but it would be a terrible shame to destroy it!" Francesca said, angrily, surprising everyone. "It would be vandalism! That garden was probably laid out when the house was built in the sixteenth century. It's historical and besides, the design isn't just the usual symmetrical pattern of hedges."

"What's so special about it?" Dip asked – not that he was particularly interested, but he was carried away by her outburst of enthusiasm.

Francesca turned to him, pleased to be able to display her knowledge. "I looked down from a window along an upstairs passage when I was seeing round the house and in *my* view –" she looked round at the others hoping for an appreciative audience, but Tony was savouring the filling which he'd separated from his piece of cake, Arthur Finch was adjusting his field glasses and Joanna was only half listening as she dealt with a small fly that had landed in her tea. "In *my* view, the design represents the plan of the house – or the house as it was when it was built.'' She sat back, waiting to see what effect her discovery would have on Dip.

''Yes – well, I suppose it's possible,'' he said politely, slightly disappointed by the revelation. He'd hoped for something more startling, though he didn't know what.

Sister Annunciata arrived at this minute – walking silently from behind the summer house. She startled them all, her long dark clothes striking an incongruous note against the bright colours of the flowerbeds and the sunlight of the afternoon.

Mrs Ware-Gillow reappeared, Arthur Finch leapt to his feet and the boys decided it was time to collect Dip's clothes and any material Miss Jardine might have found.

''I thought I had more than this but I must be mistaken – however, you'd better take what is left,'' Miss Jardine said abruptly, and passed the cloth to Tony while Dip went to rescue his clothes from the bush.

''What rubbish you boys keep in your pockets,'' Edwina laughed as she shook out the shorts. ''What's this now – I suppose it's the remains of a hankie.'' She picked up the small piece of pale material Dip had been at such pains to reach. ''Bits of paper, part of a rubber, broken pencil, a stone. Shall I throw them away for you?''

''No thanks.'' Dip pushed them back into the pocket and went to change.

*   *   *

MISS LINNIMENT seemed preoccupied when the boys called on her later. ''Thank you, put it down there, would you,'' she said absent mindedly as Tony handed her the material. ''I haven't time to do anything about it at the moment – far too much to do. What a blessing I went up there this afternoon – pass that basket would you, David. Now what should I take – bread, margarine . . . That poor woman – breaking her leg like that and no one knowing anything about it – three weeks ago! Three weeks! She must have been on the point of starvation – hardly a thing in the house to eat – cats everywhere – and the smell!'' She looked at the boys severely as if it was their fault.

''Who are you talking about?'' Dip asked, although he thought he knew what the answer would be.

69

"Why – Kate Murphy of course, and this could be a very good opportunity to get her out of that house once and for all!"

CHAPTER EIGHT

The same strange notes

SO it couldn't have been mad Kate who was playing the organ that night, unless she'd hobbled there with a broken leg, Dip thought with satisfaction. He was wondering about it while going to bed that night and suddenly remembered his precious piece of material. He took it out of his pocket and smoothed it out. It was small, ragged and cream coloured and looked as if it had been torn off something. Perhaps an old bit of sheet – but it was too silky for that. It had dried out now and he ran his fingers over the surface.

He had seen something like it before, but where? He racked his brains. It wasn't Aunt Mabel's petticoat that he'd seen flopping on the washing line – it was a different texture. And then in a flash, it came to him – he'd seen a very similar fragment in Eric Bulley's 'War Trophies Collection' which he'd reluctantly put on display at the Christmas bazaar in the village hall. A special corner of the hall had been partitioned off for First and Second World War souvenirs and objects of interest – everyone had paid 6d to go in and have a look and it had raised £2.2.6d. Eric guarded his prized collection very closely and it contained some interesting items.

Dip remembered with growing excitement a piece of parachute silk which was said to have come off the very parachute a German pilot had used when he bailed out over the Wirral after his plane had been hit by anti-aircraft fire. The pilot had been picked up and packed off to the prisoner of war camp in the Lake District, but someone had found his parachute in a field and had made a small private fortune by selling off bits to people. That was it – parachute silk and the German colour – Dip was almost sure of it; somehow he'd have

71

to check. It wasn't going to be easy; he and Eric had never seen eye to eye and he knew there'd be no co-operation from that quarter. He had an idea that Eric kept the collection together with all his home guard gear in an old shed at the back of the Bulley's cottage – heavily padlocked no doubt. Perhaps if he waited until Eric was out on one of his night exercises he'd be able to get in. Mrs Bulley, he knew, worked late hours at the NAAFI canteen at Barton Manor so she would be no problem.

If it *was* a German parachute, it might mean that someone had landed secretly – perhaps hidden away or destroyed the rest of the parachute and could even now be somewhere amongst them. A cold shiver went up his spine at the thought.

On the other hand, whoever it was could be a thousand miles away by now. It must have been only a few weeks ago, Dip reckoned. The material looked quite fresh and also if it had been there longer, a strong wind could easily have dislodged it and blown it far away.

There was that sweet paper they'd found on the marsh – the one Snipe had picked up. Gottingen was in Germany, Tony's Grandpa had said. They hadn't paid much attention to it at the time but how had it come to be there? And where was it now? Dip wished he'd kept it – it was unlikely that it would still be in Chiffchaff's pocket – or would it? He'd go and have a look now at this very moment – no time like the present, as Aunt Mabel would say.

Mr Finch kept his tweed sports jacket on a peg in the hall next to Dip's own school mackintosh and blazer. He could hear the sounds of 'I'll be with you in Apple Blossom Time' coming from the wireless in the living room and through a chink in the door, he could see Aunt Mabel unravelling some wool.

The jacket was hanging in its usual place and Dip's fingers groped around inside the pockets but there was no sign of a wrapper. Instead, he felt a smooth piece of paper in the breast pocket and pulled it up slightly. It looked like a plan or a map and a local one. He recognised one or two of the names – the Chester High Road, Marsh Lane. He pushed it back down again. Well, there was no reason why Chiffchaff shouldn't have a map – after all, his job was to visit different places and he was new to the area.

Suddenly the music from the dance band became louder. Dip

had the uneasy feeling that he was being watched. He swung round and saw Arthur Finch's beady, bright eyes regarding him. He fumbled quickly with his blazer.

"Lost something?" Mr Finch raised an eyebrow.

"Oh – yes – my pen; I thought I'd left it in my blazer but it doesn't seem to be there."

Mr Finch passed by on his way to the kitchen and Dip darted up the stairs. How long had he been observed? That had been a fiasco – he hoped he'd have more luck with the parachute.

His bedroom had a sloping ceiling – one of two attics – and was very cold in winter when there were even frosted patterns on the *inside* of the window some mornings while in the summer months it felt hot and airless. Dip went over to the window and opened it as wide as he could. He looked over to the woods and the tower of the church and thought of the strange music he'd heard there. The elm trees in the front garden obscured some of the view of the path leading up to the church but he had a clear view of part of the graveyard and the porch door. If he saw anything that looked like a nun wandering round in black he would go and investigate, he decided – no matter what time of the day or night. It couldn't have been one of the nuns from Joanna's school – they had their own chapel and their own organ. No, there was no reasonable explanation for it, unless it *had* after all been a ghost!

* * *

DIP had made casual enquiries at school during the week about the Home Guard's night exercises. Cat's-eyes Cox had seemed pleased by the interest shown in their activities – perhaps this new, serious side to the boy could be encouraged. "Would you like to help me polish up the rifles?" he'd asked. Yes, there were any number of little jobs he could find for him. Maybe this new maturity would begin to show in his algebra soon – one should never despair.

There were going to be no night exercises that week but probably one on the following Wednesday down on the marsh. It would be half term next week, Dip remembered as he gave up struggling with a long equation, and on Saturday they were going into Chester for a day out with Joanna and her father.

Tony nudged him and whispered, "Why all the questions about the Home Guard? Are you thinking of joining or something?" Cat's-eyes was scribbling another question on the blackboard but Dip just shrugged and pretended to go back to his calculations. He was going to keep his ideas to himself for a while. Tony was inclined to be sceptical – in the cold light of day he had quite convinced himself that the person in the church had been just someone practising the organ. The chocolate wrapper he'd dismissed as a pre-war one and he'd even laughed at the hint Dip had given him about the parachute. "More likely to be a piece of Mrs Ware-Gillow's bloomers," he'd suggested.

Maybe Joanna's father would take his vague suspicions more seriously – perhaps he'd mention them, just casually of course, when they met on Saturday.

* * *

THE boys had been looking forward to their day in Chester and thought it generous of Joanna to share it with them when she didn't have the chance to see her father very often. It was a sunny morning, although Aunt Mabel had insisted on Dip taking his mackintosh, and they rode their bicycles to the Hall, leaving them in the garage where Moses Jones was tinkering with an old car. Tony recognised it as a Morris 8. His grandfather had had an early model, now more or less in pieces with only the chassis remaining intact as the rest had been used for spare parts. He went over to look with interest at the bits of wire, plugs and other pieces of mechanism scattered over the floor.

"What do you want, boy?" The voice was gruff and Moses didn't bother to look up.

"Just looking. We've got a car like that – out of action now, though." The smell of oil and petrol was enticing and he moved nearer. He enjoyed pottering in a garage. The tool kit lay beside the wheel and he peered in. Dip had gone off to find Joanna.

Moses looked up at him for a minute and instead of shouting at him roughly to be off, in his usual bad tempered way, his voice became more ingratiating. "I suppose boy, you wouldn't

have such a thing as an extra one of these back at home?"
He rubbed his greasy hands on his overalls and picked up a
headlamp. "You see . . ." although the Welsh accent was thick
Tony gathered that Mrs Ware-Gillow was anxious to get the
small car back in working order as a 'run-about' as it was more
economic on petrol than the Bentley. Tony couldn't imagine
Mrs Ware-Gillow squashed into the back of the Morris with
her husband sitting beside her.

"I don't know if we've got one but I'll have a look." Perhaps
he could help Moses fix it on; his fingers itched to get at the
tool set.

"*There* you are; come on!" Joanna appeared at the door of
the garage. "We're all ready to go."

"OK. I'm coming." Moses turned back to his work without
a word.

"What was Moses talking about?" Joanna asked Tony
curiously. "I can never get a word out of him – he must save
all his conversation up for his visits to his cousins in Liverpool
– I expect they chat about the old days in the Valleys and
have Welsh sing-songs. I've just got to collect the picnic from
Edwina."

The picnic basket was ready. "My day off too," Edwina said.
She was going to the cinema to see a Western film with her new
young man, Ken, who was in the RAF and stationed nearby at
Sealand.

Mrs Ware-Gillow was standing by the Captain's Humber,
fluttering about him like a moth round a bright light.

"I'm sure Joanna appreciates your taking time off from your
h'important war work to take her out for the day and her two
friends as well." She eyed Dip and Tony with displeasure,
wondering why Joanna couldn't have invited that nice Francesca
Stewart instead.

The boys piled into the back of the car while Joanna sat in
front by her father. They waved goodbye to Mrs Ware-Gillow
who raised her pudgey hand with its fingernails painted a deep
crimson. Then they all settled back in the comfortable deep,
leather seats with sighs of pleasure.

It was a luxury to be travelling by car and a luxury to be
going anywhere at all, thought Dip. He hadn't been out of the
village since a rather hurried visit to Liverpool by train before

Christmas with his mother and Peter, when it had been cold and dark and Liverpool had been full of servicemen arriving at and embarking from the port. Crowds everywhere, barrage balloons strung up in the sky, bomb craters in the roads and ruined houses looking like giant, broken dolls' houses where fronts had been torn off, revealing staircases leading to nowhere and fragments of patterned wallpaper in rooms open to the sky. They had visited the large store, Lewis's, bombed and almost unrecognisable with its new prefabricated entrance through a narrow partitioned corridor. Peter had whined non-stop and they hadn't had enough clothing coupons with them for school trousers. The journey back had been slow, cramped and ill-lit. They'd all been relieved to get home.

Tony's thoughts were far away in the workshop he shared with his grandfather. If he could find a spare head-lamp for Moses, perhaps he would be able to borrow some of the fine tools he'd spied in the garage. He wanted them for making the prototype of his new invention – a secret weapon – the one-man submarine. The plans were only in the early stages at the moment, of course, but he was quite pleased with the complicated drawing he'd produced. The 'Swift Sub' he'd call it. No one else knew about it, not even Dip – he'd wait until it was perfected.

Joanna looked at her father as he drove along the lane. He looked tired with dark smudges under his eyes and even when he turned and smiled at them, lines of worry still creased his forehead. He asked her how she was getting on at school. ''Made lots of friends by now I expect?'' Joanna didn't want to add to his worries by telling him how she hated the convent and all the girls in it.

''And this lovely old house,'' he'd said earlier, looking round appreciatively. ''I'm sure you must be happy here. Mrs Ware-Gillow seems a kind soul.'' Joanna had just smiled and said, quite honestly, that she loved the house and her friend, Edwina, and then told her father the ghost story and about the vanishing nun, Alice Sayer.

''She sounds a friendly ghost, anyway,'' he'd smiled. ''Let's hope the story had a happy ending and that somehow she and her soldier were re-united.''

The car came out onto the main road. Captain Palmer felt

in one of the front lockers and brought out a folded map. "I thought we'd go to Chester Zoo first. Who's the map reader among us?"

"I went to the zoo a long time ago but I don't think I can remember the way exactly." Dip remembered how Peter, who'd been a baby at the time, had been sick behind a fish tank. "Perhaps I could with the map, though."

The sight of the map reminded Dip of Arthur Finch's pocket, the German chocolate wrapper, the scrap of parachute silk – he'd find a suitable moment later on, and mention them perhaps in a general sort of way to the Captain.

They found their way to the zoo quite easily, parked the car and spent an enjoyable morning looking at the different animals in the pleasant environment. They watched the sea-lions being fed, when Joanna said "I'm hungry too – let's have our picnic." There was a bench under a beech tree with the aviary opposite – the squawking parrots eyed everyone with penetrating stare from their beady orange eyes. There were some monkeys in an open cage behind them. Dip went over to them and made faces. They became excited and rattled on the netting. "I'd love a monkey as a pet," he sighed.

Joanna spread the picnic on the grass; there were tomato sandwiches, scotch eggs, a salad, plum pie made from one of Cook's precious bottles of preserved plums, and some small sponge cakes. There was a thermos of tea or dandelion and burdock cordial to drink. It looked like a feast and Joanna's father tucked in as hungrily as the others, while he told them of some of the adventures he'd had in foreign countries before the war.

'His stories are much more exciting than Aunt Mabel's *With Rod and Gun through darkest Basutoland*', Dip thought to himself.

"So that was the end of the tarantula – narrow squeak that one." Captain Palmer poured himself another cup of tea.

A middle-aged woman sitting on the bench opposite had been listening round-eyed to the last tale. "What happened to the native boy?" she couldn't resist asking. "Oh, I'm sorry to butt in, but I couldn't help overhearing."

The Captain laughed, and tied up the ends of the story. "Will you have one of these cakes?" he asked.

"Oh no, thank you – I have my own lunch here in a paper bag. I come here once a week, if I can, to see how Joey's getting on and have a little chat with him."

"Who's Joey?" Joanna asked.

"There, behind you," They turned round and saw one of the bright-eyed monkeys clinging to the bars. "He knows me, don't you, Joey boy!"

She went over to the cage. "I've adopted him, you see – it's as if he's my own monkey. There's this scheme at Chester Zoo to let people adopt an animal and pay for his upkeep. It helps, while the war's on anyway. It's a good idea, don't you think? A friend of mine has a zebra – thinks the world of it, she does. Now in some zoos, London for instance, they've had to get rid of the large wild animals like the tigers. Do you know why?"

"Because they eat too much," Tony said.

"No, it's because if the zoo were hit during a raid, the cages might be destroyed and then we'd have lions and tigers escaping and rampaging through the countryside. They'd turn savage, being frightened and hungry, and might attack people."

The animals might die in a raid too, Dip thought – although they'd nothing to do with the war, they could lose their lives in it. It affects everything, even innocent creatures like zebras, monkeys and penguins. "Can I give Joey one of these cakes – they're only small?" he asked.

"I don't think it would harm him," the woman smiled. "Look Joey, look what we've got for you."

Dip pushed half a piece of the cake through the netting. The monkey grasped it firmly with his little hand and inspected it closely – his eyebrows going up and down. He picked at the sponge with a tiny finger and popped a morsel in his mouth, rolling it round appreciatively. He swallowed it, put the rest in his mouth and reached out for another piece, eagerly.

* * *

78

"WE'LL park in the centre of Chester," Joanna's father said as they approached the city, "and we can go and have a look at the famous Roman Walls – inspiration for your history lessons!"

Joanna pulled a face. "Anyway, we're not doing the Romans, we're doing the Civil War."

"Cavaliers and Roundheads," said Tony. "Whose side would you have been on?"

"Cavaliers," Joanna and Dip said simultaneously.

"I'd have supported the King and Prince Rupert – he was very romantic looking and Cromwell should never have ordered the King's head to be cut off," Joanna said quite fiercely. "Sister Annunciata was telling us that one of the battles was fought just outside Chester."

"I'm glad to see you're absorbing some history," her father said. It was true that she was taking a much greater interest in the subject since she'd heard about Alice Sayer – it made the period come alive for her to think of the girl living at Shottington Hall during those times.

"And what about you, Tony, would you have been a gallant Cavalier in plumed hat, buckles and lace, swearing loyalty to the King?"

"No, I'd have been a Roundhead," Tony said firmly. "They were far more organised with their Model Army, and besides, what they were doing was right. Charles I thought he could do just as he liked – rule over everyone just as *he* wanted, just because he was king."

"Cromwell's lot were so dull and boring," Dip sneered.

"Who would *you* have supported, Daddy?" Joanna asked, as if to decide the argument.

"Well, it's a difficult question – loyalty to the King on the one hand and a refusal to put up with his obstinacy and the Divine Right of Kings theory on the other. You could say it was a war without an enemy. Had we been having this same conversation three hundred years ago, we'd have *had* to make up our minds. Didn't the Civil War start in 1642, Joanna, exactly 300 years ago?" Joanna looked at Dip and Tony, reflecting that they could have been on opposing sides as enemies. "Even members of the same families fought against each other," the Captain continued. "They must have wondered who they could trust. Betrayals and spying went on all the time as in every war – but how much worse when it was perhaps in your own village or even in your own house . . . the enemy within, one might say.''

Spying – the enemy within – Dip sat up. "I suppose," he began, trying to keep cool and collected about his suspicions, "there are spies at this moment – German spies in Britain – passing themselves off as normal people – mixing with us, finding out information and reporting back to our enemies?''

"Undoubtedly," said Captain Palmer. "That's why you see those posters everywhere, saying *Careless talk costs lives*. – Everyone must be on their guard.''

"Do you think even if you found something small – er – like a sweet wrapper with a German name on it, it might be suspicious?" Dip was annoyed when Tony trod hard on his foot and frowned at him. "Or a tiny piece of German parachute or something like that?''

"It could well be." The Captain caught Dip's eye in the driving mirror and smiled. "It pays for everyone to keep on their toes and do their bit.''

"Liverpool had a bad raid the other night, didn't it?" Tony asked quickly, trying to prevent Dip from making a fool of himself and elaborating any more on his clues.

"Yes. I think everyone knows about the battering the docks have been taking recently. The routes our ships are following and the times of sailings almost seem to be common knowledge." He frowned, and then his face cleared. "But we must try to put all that out of our minds for a few hours at least, mustn't we? We're having a day out today. Now – should I park here do you think?''

They were in a side street just by Northgate Street in the centre of Chester. They got out of the car, Dip feeling pleased that they were in the Captain's confidence. He knew he was right to be suspicious – he'd be even more vigilant now – that nun business needed to be cleared up as well.

"Why did you want to mention that sweet paper to the Captain?" Tony muttered as they walked along. "It was stupid – he'll think you're barmy!" He gave him a dig in the ribs.

Dip retaliated with a jab from his elbow. "That's all you know!''

The others were walking along in front and Joanna turned round. "Come along you two."

The majestic sandstone tower of Chester Cathedral rose up in front of them. "Now, that's a building I have always wanted to see," Captain Palmer said. "We'll have a look inside, and then you can show us where the city walls are."

Inside the Cathedral, it was still and quiet – their footsteps echoed on the stone floor. The lofty height of the oak rib-vaulted ceiling and the enormous arches made Dip feel very small. A few servicemen were walking round and one or two people knelt in prayer. They wandered up the nave and inspected the beautifully carved screen and choir stalls, then through the archway underneath the organ and in a minute found themselves in the cloisters where a verger was sweeping up something with a dustpan and brush. "These sailors," he was muttering to himself; "cigarette ash . . . in the cloisters!"

"How old are the stained glass windows – are they medieval too?" the Captain asked.

"Ah – no – mostly Victorian. A number of our old windows were destroyed by Cromwell's army when Chester was under siege – they've got a lot to answer for, haven't they? And Hitler's mob seems to be trying to polish off the rest. The windows on the south side and in St Werburgh's Chapel were blown out last November by incendiaries. I was fire fighting up on the tower – you never saw anything like it – raining down like fireworks!"

"Cromwell seems to be dogging our footsteps today, doesn't he?" Joanna's father said. "Chester must have seen quite a bit of action during the Civil War."

"Oh yes, indeed. King Charles himself watched the Battle of Rowton Moor from the Cathedral tower and narrowly missed being killed by a bullet fired from St John's Church as a salute. He watched from the Phoenix Tower, which is now called King Charles' Tower – you'll see it if you go up on to the walls just near here. The Chester people were loyal to the King – they were under siege from Cromwell's troops for two years, suffering terrible hardship, even resorting to eating their domestic pets – if you'll pardon my mentioning it." He coughed. Tony thought of Snipe back at home, tried to imagine eating him but couldn't – the idea was too awful.

81

"Yes," the verger went on, pleased to have an interested audience, "the King told the people of Chester to end the siege after the defeat at Rowton Moor but they held out for another nine months or so. A number of the houses were in ruins, the silver had been melted down for funds for the Royalist cause and sickness and disease were rife. One thing that *did* survive the ravages, even after the Parliamentarians had taken over, were the altar rails in St Anselm's Chapel." He smiled proudly as if they had been preserved by his own efforts. "Perhaps they were hidden away. Do go and have a look at them."

They thanked him, and moved on. Joanna had been listening avidly. The Civil War was becoming more real to her, almost as real as the war they were now living through. She could imagine the fears and tensions and the tragedies which must have occurred in this place 300 years ago. The excitement of the King's visit and the overwhelming horror of the defeat at the battle and the long drawn out misery of the siege. "Let's go and see King Charles' Tower," she suggested after they had spent a little more time in the Cathedral.

They walked over a cobbled street and up some steps onto the City Walls. Clouds were gathering overhead and a spot of rain fell. To the left, along the Walls they could see a small stone tower, with turrets and steps leading up to a door.

As they approached it Joanna felt a thrill of excitement. "We're standing on the exact spot where Charles I stood to watch the fighting – it must have been over there somewhere." She waved her hand vaguely and they all looked out onto the urban sprawl below – houses, shops, rooftops receding into distant fields and trees – Joanna could see it all and almost hear the noise of the battle, horses galloping, clash of steel, shouts and orders from the drummers.

It was starting to rain quite heavily. "I think we might see if there's a suitable film on; what do you say?" the Captain asked. "Is there a cinema nearby Dip, that you could lead us to?"

"Wizard," Dip said. He hadn't been to the cinema for ages but he remembered there was one called the Music Hall, which was near the Cathedral. Joanna was almost reluctant to leave the tower but they were getting quite wet, so they all ran along the wall, with Dip's mac over their heads as an umbrella, to the East Gate, down the steps and round the corner into St Werburgh Street, and there was the Music Hall, in a building like a chapel.

A George Formby film was about to start. The lights went down and they settled back to enjoy themselves. Once, when Dip was having a good laugh at one of George's antics, he stole a look at Joanna's father to see if he was appreciating the joke, but he was fast asleep.

"A reviving cup of tea now, I think," Captain Palmer whispered as they stood for God Save the King.

The tea shop they discovered was crowded, steamy and warm but they found a table by the window and while they ate their hot-buttered tea cakes were able to watch people hurrying to get out of the rain. It had been a marvellous day, Dip thought. He'd send the postcard he'd bought at the zoo to his parents. Joanna had borrowed her father's fountain pen and was already writing hers to Mackie, in London.

A bus drew up in the wet street outside and a number of people got off. Other people were pushing to get on. The shops were beginning to close and the pavement outside suddenly seemed crowded. Dip watched the scene idly. Tony was discussing his theory of a one-man submarine with the Captain. The window by their table was a little open to prevent the glass becoming completely steamed up and through it, above the other noises from the street, Dip suddenly heard something familiar. Something which made his skin prickle and tingle. Someone outside was whistling a few bars of unmelodic music – unharmonious and incomplete, ending on a wrong note. An eerie little refrain and haunting, the one they'd heard being played on the organ in the church. It was faint but unmistakable.

CHAPTER NINE

The creeping tide came up along the sand

DIP craned his neck and rubbed the other windows – standing up to peer out – but it was impossible to see who had been whistling. There were men, women and children, all shapes and sizes, jostling, rushing with umbrellas; the tune had stopped now – whoever it was had gone.

The others were looking at him, surprised at his sudden frantic interest in the scene outside. "Thought I saw someone I knew," he muttered.

"Quite possible," Tony said dryly, "since half the people we know come to Chester to shop on a Saturday. Nothing to get excited about."

"Some of the nuns bring a few of the boarders sometimes as a treat. Sister Annunciata was coming today, and Francesca Stewart." But Joanna didn't want to remind herself of school, and returned to writing her postcard.

The journey home was quieter – they were all sorry their day together was over. Joanna hated saying goodbye to her father and clung to him. "You'll throttle me!" he laughed, but his eyes were sad too. "Be brave – it won't be like this for ever."

After thanking Captain Palmer and arranging to see Joanna at the concert rehearsal on Thursday, the boys cycled back to Barton.

A car came down the drive – it was Moses Jones in the Bentley and out of the back got Edwina and her boy-friend. Joanna saw them through the hall window and ran to meet Edwina, thankful for a diversion now that her father had gone.

The rain had stopped but Edwina's pompadour of auburn hair looked rather crestfallen and bedraggled. "Wasn't it kind of Moses to give us a lift? There we were at the bus stop in Chester in the pouring rain and along he comes. 'Jump in' he says!'' She beamed at Moses who looked away, as if embarrassed by her effusivenesss.

"By the way, this is Ken. We all had such a nice chat coming home, didn't we? Moses is quite talkative when you get to know him,'' she added softly to the boys. "I expect he's just shy."

"Now, how about us all having a nice pot of tea in the kitchen? I must say I'm ready for one, and I'll tell you all about the Roy Rogers film we saw and you can tell me all about your day out!'' She put an arm round Joanna, and they went into the kitchen, except for Moses who stayed behind to wipe over the car.

"It's a good job the Ware-Gillows are out – I don't think they'd approve of us riding in the Bentley. Gone to visit some friends in Eccleston, that's how Moses saw us on the way back. What a downpour, wasn't it? Ow – look at my hair!'' She had caught sight of herself suddenly in the kitchen mirror.

*   *   *

AUNT MABEL looked pleased as Dip came in through the back door. "What did I tell you! Fine before seven, rain after eleven! Where would you have been without your mac?'' The little rhyme sounded all wrong but Dip couldn't be bothered to argue. That tune was going through his mind.

"Mr Finch said don't wait supper for him – he's gone into Chester to buy a book on marshland creatures. Now, before you lay the table, have a look at this book Miss Linniment dropped round for you this morning."

She handed Dip a thin volume entitled *Florence at the Front*. Opening it, he saw it was a play.

"Yes, a few members of the Women's Institute are putting this on at the concert. A scene from the life of Florence Nightingale. Miss Truce is playing the lead and Miss Linniment thinks you'd do very nicely as . . .'' Dip held his breath fearing the worst . . . "as prompter.'' This was better than he'd feared – he wouldn't mind so much if he didn't have to act.

"Do you know,'' Aunt Mabel went on with a gleam in her eye, "they've even roped in that Sylvia – the Grant's landgirl.

She has to stay in bed all the time and groan occasionally. She'll have to put white powder on her hair too." She gave a grim smile of satisfaction. She had caught the rough edge of Sylvia's tongue for not waiting her turn in the queue at the butcher's one morning, so she felt this would be a small revenge.

Dip thought the whole play sounded dreadful, but at least he would be behind the scenes, not on stage making a fool of himself. Tony had been very reluctantly persuaded to perform a few conjuring tricks and was already bitterly regretting it.

"The rehearsal's on Thursday, isn't it?" Dip asked his aunt.

"Yes, seven o'clock. Miss Linniment seemed in rather a state – she has so much on her mind. It seems that a niece of old Kate Murphy's has turned up out of the blue. Irish too, of course. She has been living in Liverpool recently and decided to look up her aunt. Apparently she's as dotty on cats as Kate is so the two of them make a good pair – she's staying at the cottage and keeping house while the leg mends. Although keeping house is an overstatement. According to Miss Linniment," Aunt Mabel lowered her voice as if afraid she might be overheard, "it seems the place is just as much a pigsty as ever. She's very cross about it all. She'd hoped to get Kate out of the cottage so she could get it properly cleaned out!"

Dip had confirmed that the Home Guard would be down on the marshes for a night exercise on Wednesday, and laid his plans carefully. He knew Eric kept his potting shed bolted but there was a small window and with any luck he might be able to ease it open and wriggle through. He planned to wait until it was really dark and take his torch with him. He prayed there wouldn't be a raid that night.

He hadn't told Tony what he was going to do. He thought he'd wait until he had some proper proof. Tony seemed preoccupied these days anyway. He'd taken the old headlamp to Shottington Hall and he and Moses had become quite friendly, swapping pieces of wire, plugs, even bits of piping. Dip wasn't interested in such things – he'd got his own preoccupations.

On Wednesday night he waited until the house was silent; then dressed in shorts, a warm dark sweater and sandals, with his torch and his precious piece of silk in his pocket, he crept out of his room. A sudden babble of words startled him but it was only Peter talking in his sleep in the next bedroom.

"Get away, get away;" his brother's voice rose into a high crescendo and then the words became incoherent again. Dip used the noise to dart along the passage and down the stairs. Aunt Mabel wouldn't stir and Arthur Finch wouldn't be likely to investigate Peter's nightmare, but he might be curious to see who was prowling round the house if he heard him.

The village was silent and dark – not a chink of light to be seen anywhere, due to the blackout, but luckily the moon came out from behind a cloud and Dip was able to find his way along the lane quite easily.

Eric Bulley lived with his mother, who worked at the NAAFI canteen, and his father, a ginger-haired, fox-faced man with a temper as short as his son's. Like Eric he was in the Home Guard, so apart from a lean and savage mongrel dog which they kept half starved, Dip reckoned the place should be empty.

The gate creaked as he opened it and mournful barking started from inside the house. The potting shed was at the back and the dog started scratching frantically at the back door as Dip walked round. He stayed still for a minute, making sure there was no one at home likely to come and see what all the noise was about. No one appeared. The potting shed was securely padlocked and the window was also firmly closed. 'Blow' – he thought – 'now what?' He felt in his pocket for his penknife and selected a small blade. With the light from his torch, he saw that the hasp for the padlock could be unscrewed if he used the blade as a screwdriver. A twinge of guilt struck him as he worked but he reminded himself of the Captain's words, "Everyone must do their bit," and it just might be of importance, this flimsy bit of material.

He was soon able to open the door. He stepped into the shed and closed it behind him. The dog sounded as though it was hurling itself against the back door in the house now and Dip was glad it couldn't escape.

Everything was meticulously tidy inside the shed. Eric's collection of 'War Trophies' as he called them was carefully laid out on a work bench and all the items were marked. There were the usual pieces of shrapnel with the dates they had been found written underneath, an army ration tin, empty cartridge cases, a bit of aeroplane control mechanism and, from the First World War, a water bottle and the *pièce de resistance*, a German helmet. Dip shone his torch into the corner of the bench and, with relief, spotted the item he had come to see. Behind a card which read, 'Piece of German Parachute', there was a scrap of pale silk. Quickly he reached about in his pocket and found his own crumpled scrap and spreading it out by the other one, compared the two. There was no doubt about it, they were identical in colour and texture. He breathed a sigh of satisfaction.

Suddenly above the noise of the dog, he heard a voice call out, "Is there anybody there?"

He switched his torch off quickly and ducked down. It must be Jim Vales the ARP warden doing his rounds and Dip wondered if he'd spotted the faint light from his torch.

"What's all the noise then?" Jim shouted, and knocked on the front door of the house. Luckily this had the effect of sending the dog running through to the front to bark there, and after a minute or two, during which Dip guessed he would be checking the locks and making sure the windows were all closed, Jim went on his way.

Dip breathed a sigh of relief, waited a few minutes and then crept out of Eric's shed, screwed back the padlock and sped away home. He let himself in to the silent house and then had a second shock. Someone was creeping down the stairs. He pressed himself back into the coats hanging in the hall, hardly daring to breathe. The steps were too heavy to be Peter's; perhaps it was Aunt Mabel fetching a glass of water. He didn't dare to move or peer out to see who it was. The steps came nearer and stopped right beside him and to his horror, he realised the coats were being moved. One was taken off its hook and then the steps padded softly away towards the back door.

He could breathe again, and he peeped out from behind Aunt Mabel's voluminous navy mackintosh to see, for a moment, a man's figure silhouetted in the doorway. It was Arthur Finch, with tweed jacket and field glasses. What on earth was he doing prowling around at this time of night? There was only one way to find out.

Taking care not to be seen, Dip followed silently behind Arthur Finch's surprisingly fast-moving figure through the

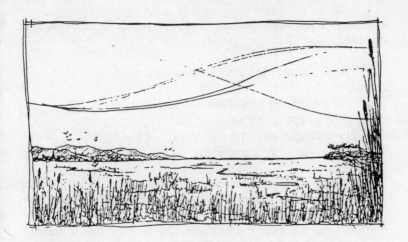

village, down Station Road, towards the marsh.

The gaunt buildings of the convent loomed up towards the right and for a moment Dip lost sight of his quarry. In the distance, he could hear the muffled sound of blank shells being fired by the Home Guard in the direction of Sealand where the aerodrome was sited – large, important and camouflaged.

In the moonlight, the marshes stretching away almost to the coast of Wales looked mysterious, with the grey-green grass of the saltings rippling in the breeze, and little pools shimmering in the reflection of the moon. Wide creeks and deep gullies intersected and wound their way snake-like through the marsh. These would soon be filled by the treacherous tidal river, cutting off anyone unwary enough to be caught on the deceptively flat and innocent-looking grass. There were many stories told of strangers to the area and animals – grazing sheep – being trapped by the tide in this way. The ghosts of excise men and coastguard officers, who had been deliberately led to their doom in the gutters and winding channels by smugglers, were said to haunt the area.

Dip had been constantly warned never to play down on the marsh. Only a few wild-fowlers knew their way round the maze of pools and creeks, and only last term Dip had learnt Charles Kingsley's poem *The Sands of Dee*, written when he was the Dean of Chester Cathedral, telling the tragic story of Mary, sent to call the cattle home, who was cut off by the tide and drowned.

> The creeping tide came up along the sand
> And o'er and o'er the sand
> And round and round the sand
> As far as eye could see
> The rolling mist came down and hid the land
> And never home came she.

The verses were full of meaning when you could look out of your classroom window and see the very sands and spartina grass stretching away before you.

There was no mist tonight and Dip was confident that he couldn't get lost. He knew where the main deep channel was and reckoned if he didn't go out beyond that, he would be perfectly safe. Anyway, he thought, old Chiffchaff certainly didn't know his way around the marsh any better than himself so he was not likely to try to walk across to Wales or anything like that. What was he up to? Perhaps he was just on a night watch for animals – he was always talking about Brock the Badger as if he were an old friend. Because of his job with the Ministry, he had access to all the land in and around Barton and had discovered at least one badger's sett. He would pop up in barns, sheds, fields and cabbage patches, ever watchful – he seemed to prowl everywhere – yes, that was the word, 'prowl'. What did anyone really know about Arthur Finch? Dip speculated. Here he was, living in their midst, able to eavesdrop, free to come and go as he pleased – and another thought struck Dip, the last time they had been walking back along the marsh footpath, Snipe had found that sweet wrapper and it had very quickly been pocketed by Finch. Why? Had it really just been to keep the path tidy? He was seized by excitement. "The enemy within" – the Captain's own words and they could mean – 'within' his own house!

At that moment Chiffchaff's distant figure could be seen hurrying from the shadow of the convent and Dip had to run from his shelter behind the group of trees crowning the sandstone headland of Barton Point, to keep him in sight. Now and then Finch stopped as if looking for something and Dip prayed he wouldn't turn around; there were no hiding places on the flat saltmarshes, only the gulleys.

They were going further and further out – the hills of Wales seemed nearer than ever before and looking back Dip saw that Barton Point and the convent were a long way away, receding into the distance. The tracks used mostly by sheep were not too difficult to follow but rain had made the ground squelchy and at the side of one gutter he missed his footing and felt himself slipping down the side, just avoiding the deep mud at the bottom.

Arthur Finch chose that moment to stop and turn round and Dip ducked his head, thankful for the safety of the ditch. He was about fifty yards ahead and appeared to be engrossed in something, but what it was, Dip couldn't see – a piece of piping possibly – certainly not a badger.

He settled himself down to watch – straining his eyes as the moon went behind a cloud. His eyelids were growing heavy and he closed his eyes for a minute to rest them thinking a jumble of confused thoughts. Was Arthur Finch a spy? Was he, perhaps, in league with someone at the convent? Had he parachuted down from a German plane, presented fake credentials in the village to enable him to come and go as he pleased near Liverpool and the air force base? Was he setting up warning lights for the evening? How did he get his information out? There were channels on the marsh deep enough for boats – boats to neutral Ireland. The strange music went through his mind – he imagined it being played by the ghost of the young woman in the portrait at Shottington Hall. Mrs Ware-Gillow was sitting listening eating a large piece of chocolate cake . . .

Dip opened his eyes with a start – one of his feet felt cold and wet. Shining his torch down he saw to his horror that the ditch was filling with water. How long had he been dozing there?

He could see no sign of Arthur Finch – he might have made his way back ages ago – half an hour or an hour even.

Dip was furious with himself – how could he have dropped off like that? Now the least he could do was to dart over to where he had last seen Finch and find out what he had been inspecting. Every move he made was uncomfortable with mud oozing out of his sandals, and some of the grass he ran over concealed more patches of mud which was almost like quick-sand, it was so soft and squelchy. It seemed to suck him down, pulling him with a force of its own.

The bank where Finch had stood was raised slightly but Dip saw that he couldn't reach it by the route he was on, as a deep channel lay between him and the mound. This channel too was filling up now. He shone his torch over the area and saw something which again could have been lead piping and something else shiny and metallic, but the torch battery was failing and the light was dim. He cursed himself again for being so stupid – he'd have to come back again in daylight.

With the flickering torch, he tried to find a firm footpath which would lead him out of the marsh. He followed what appeared to be a trodden sheep track for a while, weaving between small gutters. In the distance, he could make out the dark mass of land and it should have been a straight walk, taking just a few minutes, except for the treacherous maze of deep gullies, now filling up with the incoming tide at an alarming rate.

Soon, he couldn't see the shape of Barton Point any more – by following this track, he had come too far to the right. Panic rose in him as he realised he could be cut off by the tide if it was a high one. He struggled on, trying to retrace his steps and strike a safe path, sometimes sinking deep into the mud.

Was it his imagination or did the land suddenly look a little nearer and wasn't that the convent he could see now? He almost sobbed with relief, but almost instantly nearly fell head first into a chasm which snaked away in each direction creating an impassable barrier. It was eight feet wide and was filling with black rushing water. It was useless to try and swim across – the current was so strong it would sweep him away. He ran up and down the edge frantic and breathless, seeing the way to safety out of his reach and yet so near. In his desperation he missed his footing, stumbled on something hard and fell headlong in the grass, his torch flying out of his hand. He had tripped over a large piece of wood that was sticking up, half hidden by tall spikey grass, and Dip now realised it could be a last means of escape. It was heavy, but by scrabbling with his hands, pulling and heaving it slowly and painfully from its bed in the marsh, he eventually worked it free. It was about a foot wide, Dip reckoned, quite strong – it felt solid and heavy

– perhaps part of a wrecked boat, cast up as driftwood. The point was – would it be long enough to act as a bridge and span the channel?

When he had dragged it to the edge of the chasm he pulled it upright with a great effort, and dropped it quickly with a thud, over the gap. It almost reached to the other side but fell short by a few inches and dropped into the muddy slope opposite.

Dip realised that he would have to take the chance. Quickly he clambered onto the precariously balanced plank, dipping downwards over the fast flowing channel. The wood didn't wobble and seemed to be held fast in the mud. Taking it slowly not daring to look up, he edged his way along. He had almost reached the other side when he suddenly heard men's voices – people running, coming nearer. Someone yelled "You're almost there," but the sudden noise caught Dip off balance – he tottered, lost his footing and fell painfully into the muddy bank. Mercifully he'd been further across than he'd realised. Hands reached out to grab him and he was pulled up unceremoniously to dry land. When he looked up, he found himself gazing into the pebble lenses of Cat's-eyes Cox. It was beginning to get light and he could see four or five of Cox's platoon standing nearby.

"Well, letting your enthusiasm run away with you, were you? I suppose you thought you'd join us on our night exercises?" He spoke sternly but didn't sound too angry. Dip didn't answer – far better to let Cat's-eyes think he'd been trying somehow to join the Home Guard on manouevres, than to go into long, unsatisfactory explanations.

"Yes," Cat's-eyes continued, "luckily for you we saw your light across the marsh."

Although Dip knew he would have been able to scramble up the other side unaided, he thought it best to let Cat's-eyes believe they had rescued him.

"Thank you, sir," he muttered, hoping he sounded both contrite and humble. Then he thought of something much more important. "Did you see anyone else on the marsh besides me, Mr Cox?"

"We haven't been playing hide and seek," Mr Cox drew himself up. "We were capturing a gun emplacement. You could have been taken for one of the enemy and shot, you know. Now, I'll see you up Station Road. I won't mention this to your aunt, David, she's got enough on her plate as it is – but none of this sort of thing again, do you understand? If you want to help us, perhaps you can fill some sand bags for us at our next competition.''

That was the last thing Dip wanted but he hid his dismay by more thanks and they trudged up the road to the village.

He let himself into the house for the second time that night without making a sound. Well, at least he'd had success with his piece of parachute silk. He was muddy and shaken by his night out and glad to creep into bed.

It was late when he woke next morning. Aunt Mabel would have been cross normally, muttering about 'early to bed, early to rise', but today she was full of her own worries. Miss Linniment had called and persuaded her against her better judgement to take part in the Florence Nightingale sketch, as one of the cast had fallen ill.

Her Scottish accent became more pronounced as she commiserated with herself. ''Och I shouldna hae let the woman persuade me.''

''Oh you'll be fine, Aunt Mabel,'' Dip tried to reassure her, glad that she hadn't noticed the state his shorts were in despite a fierce brushing. ''Norah O'Brien would have jumped at the chance to act in *Play Up St Monica's*.'' One of Aunt Mabel's own sayings now came to him in a flash; ''You never know what you can do, till you try!''

She looked at him quickly to see if he was making fun of her but he kept a straight face so she just said ''Aye – aye.''

He spread some plum jam on his bread and margarine, then enquired casually, ''Where's Mr Finch? Has he gone to poke and pry round some more gardens?''

''No,'' Peter answered with his mouth full. ''He's gone to Liverpool or somewhere for the day. I had a terrible dream last night – about rats – I'll tell you all about it.'' While Peter's description of his nightmare went on, Dip was having his own thoughts. There was definitely something strange going on. He didn't know what, but decided it was time to tell Tony about the parachute and Chiffchaff. He would mention it tonight at the rehearsal.

"And so this huge rat with bright red eyes started creeping out of the hole, very slowly and . . ." just before he got to the exciting bit Peter choked on a crumb.

CHAPTER TEN

Letter from the past

THE rehearsal was due to start at eight o'clock. "Far too late," Aunt Mabel had grumbled. She had been given a small piece of paper on which her lines in the play were written and she kept repeating them over and over again as they walked up to the village hall. Peter almost had to be dragged along – he was coming in the capacity of Assistant Stage Manager.

"You'll just have to be a helping hand to everyone – running errands and tidying up – that sort of thing – a general dog's body," Miss Linniment had said brightly, but Peter had looked dubious.

By eight o'clock Dip could hardly keep his eyes open and was glad to sit in the wings waiting for the short play to commence. He had been given a book with all the parts but he put it down and yawned loudly.

"Do that again." Tony ran up to where Dip was sitting. "I think I could use that yawn in my act." He produced an old leather case and out of it took a couple of ping pong balls.

"Now, when I twist your ear, like this" – Dip let out a yell – "you open your mouth and I'll produce these like this, voila! Well, perhaps it needs a bit of practice," he admitted as the balls slipped out of his hand and bounced away. "I've had a good idea – I'm going to ask Joanna to be my assistant – conjurors always have them – she can borrow one of Mum's frilly blouses or she could wear her red shiny long dress, but it might be a bit big for her . . ."

Tony's animation only made Dip feel more tired – he wanted to tell him about last night but Tony was off again before he could get a word in.

"And another thing," his eyes were shining. "Scruffy

Simpson said I could borrow his white mice. I'm going to produce them out of a hat." He foraged around in his case and brought out not a black top hat, but an old tweed cap of his grandfather's. Dip eyed it sardonically. "I think you'd be better sticking to your card tricks."

"Oh – it'll be all right – look, I've made a special place for them here – they can breathe and everything. Scruffy said he'd bring them round tonight so I can get the feel of them."

"Quiet everyone!" The shrill tones of Miss Linniment rang out from the main body of the hall. She clapped her hands to stop the buzz of conversation still going on among the choir.

A small girl played a long monotonous piece on the piano, which was badly out of tune. She had trouble turning the pages of her music and Peter was asked to help. He strode onto the stage red in the face, his eyes glassy with embarrassment.

"Now – now," hissed the girl and Peter turned over two pages at once. No one else would have noticed but she insisted on going right back to the beginning again.

Mr Martin, the popular village butcher, was due to appear next, with a monologue he'd written. But he'd been playing in a cricket match and hadn't arrived yet, so they went straight into 'The Nuns' Chorus'. Some of the women in the choir had brought their costumes and were wearing them.

Miss Truce was working the curtains and opened them with a flourish on the strangely ill-attired group. The accompanist struck the opening chords and the choir launched into a full-throated rendering of their song.

Dip watched them thoughtfully – any one of them could pass for a nun, dressed like that. He remembered the fuss about the missing costume. Perhaps no one had made a mistake counting them. Maybe someone had deliberately taken one, or at least a length of the material?

Joanna had arrived and was waving to him from the opposite side of the stage. Over her arm she carried a bundle of aprons which Miss Jardine had reluctantly lent for the cast of the Florence Nightingale play.

'The Nuns Chorus' had ended with Miss Linniment triumphantly attaining the final high notes. Little groups of people waiting for their turn clapped politely as she stepped forward to bow and smile. She signalled to Miss Truce to close the curtains on the others. This was accomplished by a series of jerks, and then a few introductory notes on the piano launched Miss Linniment into 'Ole Man River', more suited to a rich baritone voice than her quavering soprano. As she extolled the virtues of the Mississippi, still wearing her nun's costume, Dip could feel Tony shaking silently beside him and glancing round, saw his friend's eyes wet with tears of laughter. He dug him sharply in the ribs but it seemed to make him worse and in desperation he now reached for his long line of coloured handkerchiefs which he stuffed into his mouth in an effort to stop himself laughing out loud.

". . . just keep rolling along . . ." sang Miss Linniment, hands pressed together earnestly. Tony thought he would choke. It was infectious and both boys had tears running down their cheeks as she stepped behind the curtains at the end of the song. She eyed them sharply. Tony started pulling the handkerchiefs out of his mouth – red, yellow, blue . . .

"Practising already? Well, you can go on next if you like."

Tony tried to compose himself. "Oh, I'm afraid I'm waiting for a friend – he's bringing some . . . some of my equipment."

There was a short break in the rehearsal. Some of the nuns' habits were exchanged for aprons. Sylvia, the landgirl, strode in looking cross, wearing a short dark-haired wig and a moustache, and Joanna ran across the stage to the boys.

Tony asked if she would act as his assistant and she nodded her head and smiled. "What do I have to do?"

While he was explaining, the vicar came over. "I believe I'm giving you a lift home, young lady. I have to see Mrs Ware-Gillow about some flowers she promised my sister for the confirmation service next week."

"Oh, yes, thank you," Joanna said.

"How did you get here this evening – by bike?" Dip asked her.

"No, I had a lift from Moses Jones – it's his afternoon off but he had to take Mr Ware-Gillow to Liverpool so he was going to see some cousin called Griffith."

While there was a lull in the rehearsal Dip thought it would be a good opportunity to tell the others about the previous night's adventures and he said in a conspiratorial whisper, "Listen, there were some strange goings on . . . last night on the marsh. We ought to meet somewhere – somewhere quiet. I know – how about your shelter at the Hall tomorrow afternoon?'' Tony and Joanna were all ears but at that moment Scruffy arrived, out of breath.

"Sorry I'm late," he said, cheerfully, opening the small box he was carrying to reveal three white mice. "I took a short cut round the back of the church." He put his finger into the box and tickled one of the mice. "There were strange noises inside – sort of music that wasn't music – weird – the door must have been open. I didn't stop to see who . . . oops!" One of the mice didn't enjoy being tickled and took a flying leap out of the box. There was sudden pandemonium among Florence Nightingale's nurses and patients. Tony and Joanna went searching between people's feet and Scruffy darted through the curtains.

Meanwhile Dip took this opportunity to race out of the stage door. Scruffy's words had set his pulses racing. That music again! He just hoped that whoever it was playing the organ would still be there. He ran up the churchyard path and stopped in the porch, bent double and panting. There was no sound. He pushed the heavy door which was already ajar, and peered in but the church was completely empty; there was no one there. The door to the bell tower was open. As he was running up the spiral stair to the bell ringing chamber, something caught his eye. It was the loop of bell ropes. They were swaying slightly from side to side. – Undoubtedly someone had been here very recently. But whoever it was had already slipped away. A weary and puzzled Dip made his way back to the rehearsal.

*　　　*　　　*

THAT night there was another raid. A short one, but very close. The aerodrome at Sealand was hit by incendiaries and fires started up. If the fires had not been put out quickly, they could have acted as guiding lights for the next raid, when the RAF station would probably have been destroyed.

As he wheeled his bicycle out onto the road next day, Dip hoped the others would turn up for their rendezvous. He was half regretting the arrangement now, thinking his time might have been better spent in keeping track of Arthur Finch or at least going down to the marsh in daylight to see if he could find what had absorbed him on Wednesday night. However, Tony soon appeared, and they started off together for the Hall.

"Those mice were really good – I've just got to get the timing right . . ."

"Never mind the mice! What about the raid last night? What about that organ music?" Something clicked in Dip's mind as he spoke the words. Those two things seemed to go together – had gone together before. First the music in the church and shortly afterwards a raid. Tony's grandfather had heard it first and there'd been a raid that night.

"Oh – go on," Tony scoffed, as Dip tried to explain, "you're imagining things. You see sinister goings-on everywhere. Now it's that old yarn about the Nazi spy dressed up as a nun, isn't it? You really believe it, don't you? You want to be careful, you know; remember the trouble we got into when we reported that artist?"

"But the bell-rope was still swinging when I got there. I tell you someone had been there all right and . . ."

They looked towards the church and the bell tower and to their amazement saw, wandering among the tombstones, a nun – her black habit blowing slightly in the breeze.

Dip blinked hard and dropped his bike against the wall. "What's she doing there? Let's go and see if it's a genuine one."

They climbed the track up to the churchyard and hid behind a large granite monument to get a better view.

"It's the Sister from the convent – the one who came with Francesca to the Hall when we played tennis." They watched for a moment as she paused in front of a large grave – a horizontal sandstone slab, uneven and very old. She seemed to be peering at the lettering. "I thought they were all Roman Catholics at the convent. I wonder why she's here – at St Nicholas," Dip whispered. Tony shrugged his shoulders.

"Ah – good afternoon." Mr Truce had come through the porch and was greeting Sister Annunciata.

"It all looks very fishy to me," Dip persisted as the two of them ran back from the churchyard and climbed on Dip's bike. They sped down Shottington Lane – Tony sitting on the saddle with his legs out and Dip pedalling furiously.

Joanna's half term had started that day and she was already in the shelter – and while she'd been waiting she had brewed some tea. The smell of Mr Ware-Gillow's cigar still lingered in the air from the night before and mingled with the heavy floral scent favoured by his wife.

"Edwina was terribly worried," Joanna said when they were drinking their tea. "Her boy-friend, Ken, is stationed at Sealand but it's all right – he managed to ring her this morning from a call box – and they've almost put out the fires too. We seem to be having an awful lot of raids round here – almost as bad as London!"

Dip remembered Captain Palmer's words about "the battering of the docks", and how the sailing times of the convoys seemed to be common knowledge, and now launched right into his suspicions, despite Tony's disbelief.

"Look – there was that missing nun's costume, remember – someone could have pinched it – ideal camouflage round here with the convent and even the chorus in the Women's Institute concert. Then Tony and I found that sweet paper with the German wrapper – no, it wasn't an old one," he added, catching Tony's eye. "There's that strange music up at the church which is always heard just before or during a raid and also *this*!" Out of his pocket he brought the scrap of parachute silk, explaining how he'd compared it with the German one in Eric's shed, and going on to tell about his adventures on the marsh following Arthur Finch.

"I agree with Dip," Joanna said solemnly after hearing his story. "There is something strange going on. There could be . . ." she paused for dramatic effect, "an enemy in our midst! But – shouldn't we tell someone who'd take it seriously – the police or Home Guard . . .?

"Well, it's a bit difficult . . . We had a bit of trouble before, when we reported an artist – how were we to know he was just sketching trees – but it means they're not going to believe us in a hurry, you see."

"What do we do now, then?" Joanna asked.

"We should make a list of suspects and keep a careful watch on them." Dip pulled an old envelope and a stub of pencil out of his pocket.

"Key suspect . . . Arthur Finch," he wrote at the top. "We know nothing about him – he prowls around all over the place finding out everyone's business. Vanishes whenever he likes – he had access to black costumes when Aunt Mabel was sewing them."

"What about the music, though?" Tony had been impressed by the parachute silk and was beginning to be convinced in spite of himself.

"Perhaps he or she dresses up in black and plays on the organ to frighten people," Dip improvised, "to pretend he's a ghost, to act as a decoy or something . . ." He felt baffled himself on this point.

"And that reminds me – I heard that same tune on Saturday when we were in Chester with Joanna's father. It was being whistled, but I couldn't see who it was." He whistled the tune himself, as if it would somehow bring an answer.

"Then there's suspect number two . . . Sister Annunciata. I'm sorry, Joanna, I know you like her but she's Austrian and has her own loyalties. We saw her up at the church today and," he added triumphantly, "I remember you saying she was in Chester on Saturday with a group from your school."

"Oh, it couldn't possible be her – she's . . ."

"Then suspect number three," Dip continued hurriedly. "Old Kate Murphy or niece or both."

The others looked surprised. "Well, she's Irish and Ireland's neutral – easy to get information from there. You could keep a boat down on the marshes and sail over from here. The niece has contacts in Liverpool, and they live near the church. We really can't overlook *anyone* – even old Cox – he might have ulterior motives for his Home Guard activities – and he knows the marsh like the back of his hand."

"Oh, surely not Cat's-eyes," Tony protested, but they all felt uneasy.

"It could even be . . . Miss Linniment," but the others found this too far fetched and laughed.

"I'll dog Chiffchaff's footsteps – out of school, anyway, and you," Dip said to Tony, "can keep a watch on Kate's cottage and report anything suspicious."

"Thanks a lot – that's not going to be easy with Snipe and all those cats."

"Jo, you can observe Sister Annunciata and . . ."

From somewhere up in the garden came a muffled and distant shout. "Johanna!"

"It's Mrs Ware-Gillow! She mustn't see us coming out of here." Joanna crept through the open door and up to the garden to see if the coast was clear.

"It's all right." They came up into the daylight and saw Moses pottering about among the roses. There was no sign of Mrs Ware-Gillow, so they walked over to the house.

"Oh there you are, Johanna!" Mrs Ware-Gillow gave one of her cross smiles as she saw Joanna in the hall with the two boys. "The Reverend Truce is here. For some reason or another," she lowered her voice slightly, "he wants to go picking around those old papers up in the attic – goodness knows why – some book he's writing or something. Anyway, I'm certainly not running up and down stairs rummaging in dusty piles of old books, so I want you to show him where they are, Joanna."

"Yes, he did mention that he'd like to look at them when he brought me back after the rehearsal yesterday," Joanna agreed.

Mrs Ware-Gillow swept into the drawing room. "Ah, Vicar, here we are now." The smile lost its cross look. "Johanna will escort you up to the attic – I'm afraid I can't be of much help – 'istory was never one of my strong points."

The two boys waited until Mrs Ware-Gillow had gone back to the drawing room and then followed Joanna and the vicar up the stairs. The attic looked as if no one had been over the threshold since the last time they were there. The leather straps of the trunk were still unbound as they had left them. The vicar's eyes gleamed as they pushed back the lid and revealed the jumble of papers and documents inside.

"This history of the parish I'm attempting to write," he said, picking over one or two of the pages lying on the top, "needs a lot of research. There are gaps in the history of the Hall that I'd like to fill in. You see, Sir William Sayer died during the Civil War in 1645; his daughter, who should have inherited the property, appears to have vanished into thin air and a distant cousin inherited instead, some time later. She'd become a nun, or almost a nun, apparently. Perhaps," he added, with a smile, "She's the one who features in the ghost story you were telling me about?"

Dip remembered something he'd wanted to ask. "Our church in the village is Church of England. Could it have been a Catholic one during the Civil War?"

"No, no. After Queen Elizabeth and her *Via Media* policy, the official religion of the country was Church of England, although there were still religious difficulties for years to come. But no, our own St Nicholas would not have been Catholic at that time."

The Sayer family were Catholics and while the ghost of Alice Sayer might well haunt the Hall, it would be unlikely that she'd appear at St Nicholas, Dip reasoned. That ruled out the ghost theory. At the back of his mind he'd still been half ashamed to admit that what he'd seen might have been supernatural, so now he felt relief.

"Mind you," the vicar continued, "our little church holds interest for people of other denominations too – the Quakers' graves and, of course, Father Plessey who was family priest to a later branch of the Sayer family, poor man. He lived during troubled times and was accused of conspiracy. He was hung, drawn and quartered at Chester, in 1679; I think I've got my date right. His body was taken back to the Hall and later buried at Barton, but no one knows exactly which grave is his. All the old sandstone slabs are weathering away and the lettering is indistinct. There is some talk of canonising Father Plessey. That means making him a saint. In fact, this very afternoon, one of the nuns from the Sacred Heart – I expect you will know her," he turned to Joanna, "was in the graveyard looking for his tomb."

"Sister Annunciata," Dip reminded her.

"Yes, she was most interested and very knowledgable about him – apparently he had family connections in the same part of Austria that she comes from and she is writing an article on him for your school magazine. I told her to be sure and let me know if she discovers his burial place," he laughed; "so many have searched in vain. And now," he said, "to work!"

That seemed to knock another of Dip's theories on the head – two in the space of five minutes. Still, he supposed it was helpful in a negative sort of way.

They sifted through a pile of the papers, carefully sorting

through old bills, receipts, faded photographs, turning them over eagerly.

"Here are some plans of the house – they look like the proposed extensions which were carried out in 1763." The vicar said excitedly "This is a real treasure trove!"

Dip went across to the window and looked out over the surrounding countryside and the garden down below. Bonfire smoke was drifting about; Mrs Ware-Gillow was cutting some early yellow roses. A peaceful scene, but he scowled. Somewhere there was fighting going on – people were being killed. Here he was spending his time in an attic looking at useless old papers when he should be *doing* something. He watched a bee, which had somehow got into the room, banging itself against the window in a vain effort to get out and felt sympathy with it. That was just how he felt – frustrated, buzzing inside with anger. He'd wanted to talk to the others about his suspicions and organise a proper look out. The vicar's arrival had ruined his plans. The others were talking away quietly in the corner – as if what they were doing was interesting!

He opened the window with difficulty and let out the demented bee. His eye wandered down to the knot garden. He supposed it would be dug up soon for vegetables. He grinned briefly, remembering that bossy girl, Francesca, and the way she'd been furious at the suggestion. The box hedges had been clipped recently by Moses and looking down at the pattern they made, he remembered Francesca's remark about the design being based on the plan of the house. Yes, it did look rather like that – the hedges represented the walls of the rooms – the drawing room was obviously that large oblong facing south-west where they grew parsley and mint . . .

"Dip, come and see what we've found," Joanna called, pointing at some yellowing documents the vicar was holding. The others seemed quite excited, even Tony.

"This is even better than I'd hoped for!" Mr Truce said. The papers had been wrapped in the satin which the children had noticed when they were collecting the blackout material. The vicar read them to himself for a minute or two.

"It seems that Colonel Sayer's mother was quite an historian. She was trying to put together a family history, during the last century. She came across old bills, receipts, family letters, but her greatest find appears to be a letter written by the Alice Sayer who became a nun – it was concealed in a very old herbal book in the library and had never been delivered. Mrs Sayer writes all this in her little introduction.''

"You mean she actually found a letter written by Alice Sayer!" Joanna repeated excitedly. "Perhaps it will solve the mystery of what happened to her – *do* go on!" she implored.

"The book, *Swinburn's English Herbal* is preserved as I found it," the vicar read, "and I have placed it with all other documents.''

"It must be in the trunk!" Tony said excitedly and delved back in among the assortment of papers.

"Careful now," the vicar admonished. "These things have lain hidden for many years – they must be preserved for posterity.''

So very carefully they sorted through the pile, and finding a wooden box at the bottom of the trunk opened it and peered inside. The ancient leather-bound book inside bore the title *Swinburn's Complete English Herbal*.

Joanna drew it out gingerly, as if it might dissolve at any minute into a thousand pieces.

"This book is a treasure in itself," the vicar said, turning a page or two. There were finely drawn illustrations, recipes for syrups and syllabubs, cures for the ague, but all written in a language which was difficult to follow and interspersed with Latin.

Towards the end, the book, seemed to bulge a little and fell open naturally at 'Rosemary for Remembrance' and there lay a small sheaf of parchment with faint writing in brown ink.

"It must be Alice's letter!" They gazed at it solemnly, thinking of the young woman who had written it, feeling guilty at the thought of prying into those secret thoughts even after all this time.

The vicar took the pages up with trembling hands. "This old English is a little hard to decipher. I have some experience of it but . . . well, we'll have a try . . .''

CHAPTER ELEVEN

The secret of the knot garden

'MY own true beloved,' the letter began. It was dated September 1645. 'This is my last visit to my father's house before I take my final vows. If we can never be together as man and wife I shall serve God at the Convent of the Blessed Mary.

'It doth grieve me sorely that we must part. This dreadful war. How long must it continue? I know you believe God is on your side but we must show loyal support to our King. No County of its size has seen more fighting and I fear we have not yet seen the worst. This siege of Chester cannot continue – what will happen?'

Slowly and painstakingly the vicar read and translated, with the children hanging on every word. They heard how Alice had had a grievous quarrel with her father who had wished her to marry the son of a 'Good Catholic friend'. How she had decided to renounce the world and become a nun. How an artist had visited the Hall and painted her protrait. 'Twill be some companye for my father when I am no longer here,' she had written sadly.

'My trusted maid, Deb, will see this reaches you through our loyal and true friend Blacksmith Bradshaw. I pray for you with all my heart and beseech Our Lady that we may one day meet again in Heaven . . .'

The letter was not finished but ended on two desperate words 'someone comes . . .'

The hasty hiding of the letter in the herb book could be imagined. Who had disturbed her and how was it that the letter had never been delivered by the 'trusted Deb'?

They felt a sense of disappointment.

''Well, a truly amazing discovery but I'm afraid we are no

further on in the mystery of what became of her. I don't suppose we shall ever know." The vicar sighed.

"September 1645, the date of the letter," Joanna burst out. "That was the date of the Battle of Rowton Moor."

"You're quite right," the Reverend Truce beamed at her; "maybe someone came in to tell her the news, or perhaps it was her father come to say that the King had arrived in Chester and he must go to the City and show his support, while he could still gain entrance by the North Wales road or by the river."

Heavy footsteps came creaking along the passage and a moment later Mrs Ware-Gillow's plump red face appeared round the door. She paused to catch her breath. "Well," she said with mock joviality, "still poking among all the dust and cobwebs?"

The vicar glanced at his watch. "Good gracious is that the time?"

"I thought you might like a tiny glass of sherry before you go?" she puffed.

"Thank you, dear lady, but I must be on my way. But I do have a great favour to ask of you – would it be possible for me to borrow these for a few days for a little extra study?" He pointed to the pages which had been written by the Victorian Mrs Sayer.

"Take the whole trunk load as far as I'm concerned," Mrs Ware-Gillow laughed shortly; "what good's a pile of old papers, I ask you!"

"No, no, no – these must stay where they belong as part of the house, or perhaps they should be in the archives – they are worth a good deal to historians." He followed Mrs Ware-Gillow, turning back to ask the children to put the other items back very, very carefully.

"It's strange to think," Dip said slowly, interested in spite of himself, "strange to think that she actually wrote all that here in this house 300 years ago; gives you a creepy feeling somehow."

"But the house has changed a bit – those plans, 1760 something, show the alterations," Joanna said.

"Your friend, Francesca, said the knot garden probably showed the plan of the original house – I was looking at it before – come and have a look. I'm afraid to say, she was probably right!'' Dip pointed to the pattern of hedges and they studied the design.

"Yes – there's the drawing room – that must be the library.'' Joanna traced the different rooms, pointing her finger. "It doesn't seem to have changed all that much. Perhaps just the kitchen area was modernised in the eighteenth century and the façade of the Hall changed a little.''

"What's that bit on the left?'' Tony asked.

"It looks like part of the library but it's not quite right – an extension perhaps – it would make it a different shape. Actually it's where the little summer house is now – where the old croquet set is kept and deck chairs and things. I'm not allowed in there. Mr Ware-Gillow keeps his orchids in there and a vine.''

The plan of 1763 was lying on the top of the papers in the trunk and Tony picked it up. "It looks as if they altered the gardens at the sides – added some steps and a garden temple and changed the level of the terrace.''

"Look!'' Joanna said, scrutinising the plan again. "Where the library is now – they've called it Chapel/Library. Don't you see, it must have been the family's private chapel and in 1763 perhaps it wasn't used so much and they decided to change it into the library. I always feel the room is different somehow – it's peaceful and – and . . .'' she tried to find the right words.

Dip wasn't very impressed by all this. The afternoon hadn't turned out a bit as he'd hoped it would. They seemed to have spent hours pouring over musty old papers when they should have been organising themselves into a vigilante society for more urgent up-to-date matters, and besides he was beginning to feel very hungry. What day was it? – Friday. There would be macaroni cheese for supper.

"I'm off,'' he said shortly. Well, if the other two weren't interested, he'd have to be on his mettle and do the sleuthing by himself, even if it did mean being in three places at once.

"Hang on a minute,'' Tony said. He was still bending over the plan. "If this used to be the chapel here,'' he stabbed his finger at the drawing, "then I wonder what the small bit added on used to be. The bit they altered and paved over.''

"Perhaps it was where the organ used to be, or the family

pews or where the priest put on his vestments. I'm sure there's nothing remaining of it now."

"I'd like to see, though," Tony said. "It'd be interesting to find a bit of the old foundations or something."

"I'm going home, I'm hungry," Dip muttered, fed up with all this irrelevant talk. Where was their sense of urgency? Didn't they realise that a Nazi spy was in all probability living among them and sending back information? Of course it was an ideal place here – near to Liverpool, the vital port, and by the RAF station, convenient for neutral Ireland . . .

"Well, let's at least have a quick look on our way back," Tony persisted.

"It's 'out of bounds' really, with all those nectarines and orchids and the vine. There's even a small paraffin heater which they use there in the winter when its frosty. I've only looked through the window. Mr Ware-Gillow sometimes goes there after lunch. He pretends the flowers and things are his chief hobby, but really he just goes in for a sleep."

They ran downstairs and out into the garden. No one was about – the air was still and fragrant with the smell of cut grass. The paving on the terrace round the house was old and uneven, little rock plants grew between some of the slabs. By the summerhouse, which was built onto the main wall of the Hall, the paving was even more disjointed – sizeable gaps appeared in two or three places which would have to be filled in with more soil and small plants.

"The land mine in January caused this damage and broke some windows," Joanna explained. "Edwina said it was dreadful – as if the whole earth was shuddering she said, but of course, you'd know all about it."

It had been dreadful. The vibrations and shock which had rocked the church had seemed like an earthquake to Dip – he had never experienced anything like it before and never wished to again. The mine had been unloaded by an enemy plane, intending it no doubt for Liverpool. Evidently the German had been chased by a Hurricane and the crew had dropped it in a panic. Fortunately, it had landed in a field bordering on the woods and no one had been hurt, but it had been a near thing, causing other more subtle and damaging side effects. Cracks had appeared in buildings, including the Church bell tower, tiles came off roofs, chimney pots were made unsafe. Mrs Jellicoe had gone deaf and Tony's grandfather's hens hadn't laid for weeks.

The summerhouse itself seemed sturdy enough, Victorian Gothic but of a mellow brick which blended with the rest of the building, and arched windows.

Inside it smelt lush and leafy. A few tomato plants in pots stood next to a row of what Joanna thought were the nectarines, and by itself standing aloof on its own shelf was something rare and exotic.

Tony read out 'Dendrobium Phalaenopsis' with some difficulty from the label on the pot.

"It's the precious orchid – the one Mr Ware-Gillow says is going to win the Queen of the Show cup at the flower show."

They looked at it in awe – it was beautiful – arrogant and aristocratic with soft rose petals and dark purplish red inside. Tony felt drawn towards it in its cool perfection – he lifted the pot carefully to look down into the petals.

"Someone's coming – put it back," Joanna hissed frantically, as they heard footsteps approaching the summerhouse.

In his eagerness to replace the pot as quickly as he could, Tony almost lost his balance. The precious orchid rocked precariously on the edge of the shelf for a second, and it seemed certain that it would crash down to the floor, but to everyone's relief it settled back and they breathed again, before ducking down among the old croquet mallets and pile of deckchairs.

The footsteps paused for a minute outside and then continued on again round the terrace. Dip leant back heavily against the deck chairs. "Phew!" He leaned too hard and the pile collapsed with a clatter. No one came to see what the noise was and they tried to stack them up again against the wall.

Behind where the deck chairs had been propped, a gaping hole revealed itself in the yorkstone paving. The slabs were a continuation of the terrace outside. "I suppose that's from the land mine as well," Joanna remarked looking at it. The hole seemed even larger than the ones outside. Tony stood over it and looked into the cavity, then he bent down and scrutinised it more closely.

Dip's stomach began to rumble – he'd had enough. "Come on, let's go."

"Fetch me a large stone or something heavy," Tony commanded, ignoring Dip's remark.

"What are you doing now?" Dip grumbled; but Tony wasn't listening, he was lying on the ground putting his hand and arm into the space.

Joanna quickly found a large piece of sandstone which Tony took, and to Dip's surprise dropped down the hole. There was a moment or two before they heard it land with a muffled thud. Tony looked up triumphant. "I thought so! Here, help me move this!"

Pulling at the slab with all their strength they managed to drag it slightly to one side. They looked at each other and then at the yawning black hole beneath. A musty smell rose up out of the earth.

"What is it – why does it go right down like that?" Joanna looked puzzled.

"I'm not sure, but I'm going down to have a look! If this summer house was built over a part of the old chapel – a priest's ante-room or something, perhaps this was a secret hiding place – somewhere for him to hide himself away when things became dangerous – you know, religious persecution!" He brought the words out with a flourish. "Who's coming to have a look?" He looked down into the hole, his hands grasping the edges.

"There seem to be some old steps!" He lit a match from a box he kept in his pocket. "I'm going down." He stepped backwards down the uneven, stone steps until he reached the bottom. The others followed, after Dip had pulled the deck chairs over the cavity in case someone should suddenly surprise them.

Tony lit another match and they looked round. The small cave-like room had been hacked out of the sandstone and seemed damp and claustrophobic.

"I shouldn't like to be cooped up in here for long," Joanna said, shivering.

"I bet the old priests were jolly glad of this place if their enemies were after them. Look at this pile of earth and rubble on the ground. It must have fallen in after the land mine. The Georgians probably didn't even know about this place when they laid their terraces. Just think – " Tony stopped short and they all froze as they heard footsteps overhead, sounding nearer and nearer. Someone had come into the summerhouse.

They stayed quite still while movements were heard above them – sounds they could identify like a watering can being filled, plant pots being moved around, plants being watered. Then a pause while perhaps the tomato plants were being tied up or the orchid being admired; whoever it was seemed in no hurry. They might be trapped down there for ages.

Dip's eyes had grown accustomed to the darkness which was relieved only by a thin shaft of light from between the deck chairs. The walls of the rough cave-like cell were not complete and an even blacker aperture appeared to have been hollowed out at one side.

While the watering can was being filled again, he nudged the others and beckoned. Carefully and silently he led the way into the gloom. It wasn't another room but what seemed to be a passage. Feeling their way along, they crept a few yards before

Tony thought it safe to light another match.

The flame flickered and cast grotesque shadows on the dark walls – it stayed alight long enough to show that the passage continued.

"Shall we go on?" Tony whispered.

"Yes, we must see where it comes out," Dip answered.

Clinging together, they pressed forward, stopping every now and then to light another match. Abruptly Tony stopped. They seemed to have come to a dead end. He had his arm stretched out in front of him and it had come in contact with the hard rock. Dip and Joanna stumbled into him.

Tony felt for his matches – only a few left – and struck one of them. The passage had widened out.

"I've lost my sense of direction completely; are we on our way to Chester, do you think? Or will we come out in Wales?" Joanna asked.

"We'll be lucky if we come out anywhere," Dip replied gloomily. "How do we know if it ever comes out? Perhaps they got fed up with making it and gave up."

"I don't think we've come very far really – it just seems like it because we are creeping along so slowly."

The passage was almost octagonal at this point and seemed to have rough seats cut out of the rock. A ledge ran round at a higher level.

The match flickered and almost died – but not before the three children had simultaneously become aware of a chill in the air and a new movement in the semi-darkness. There was a shape in the very corner they had started to edge towards. A large, menacing black figure loomed up, robes billowing – a figure with no face moving, moving towards them. A black shape, dark and sinister.

Then the match went out and they were plunged into total blackness.

CHAPTER TWELVE

The night of the concert

JOANNA'S scream of terror seemed to reverberate round the walls, echoing their terror. Dip was too paralysed by fear to make any sound at all. He felt Tony clutch at him frantically. The match box had dropped. They clung together in the dark, not knowing what was going to happen to them. The silence after the scream was even more frightening.

"The match box," Tony whispered urgently at last, "I must find it." He bent down and felt about on the rough ground.

"It's the nun – it's Alice's ghost, I tell you," Joanna was whispering hoarsely, gripping Dip's arm so tightly that it hurt. Dip said nothing but silently agreed that it was probably a nun, but more likely to be the figure he'd seen playing the church organ. But what was the figure doing while they clung together in fear in the darkness? Was it waiting like a panther, ready to spring at them? Or had it taken fright and glided swiftly and silently down the passage to . . . where? They didn't even know where it led.

It seemed ages before Tony found the box and with shaking fingers struck another match. They hardly dared to look. Joanna put an arm over her head and peered through half closed eyes – then she let out another cry and Dip pressed himself hard against the stony wall as they saw that the figure had not moved.

Tony's voice came out, not sounding at all as it usually did but weak and croaky. "Who . . . who are you?" he challenged.

The skirts rustled softly but no answer came.

Dip made a move towards it in spite of Joanna's frenzied grip. Something about the robe looked familiar. He recognised the material. Aunt Mabel had sat sewing it often enough

115

recently; it was the blackout material worn now by members of the nuns' chorus.

The others stared in horrified amazement as he broke away from Joanna's hold and gave the robe a sharp tug. It billowed out again, shadows leapt up on the roof of the tunnel and then suddenly Dip was enveloped in soft inky blackness.

Joanna turned her head away quickly, unable to stand any more until Tony said gently "It's all right – look!" She turned round slowly and saw Dip disentangling himself from a mound of fabric.

"Look, it was hanging from this hook, and there's something underneath it." From under the folds he grasped a small cardboard box in which were carefully wrapped a compass and a yellow oilskin pack. Deftly he undid it and found emergency food rations – dehydrated tubes of condensed milk; chocolate, biscuits, tins of bully beef.

Tony bent down, holding the last match right to the very end. "What does it mean?"

"I'm going to put it all back as we found it," Dip said grimly. "Someone's using this place as a secret hideaway."

A sudden draught of air blew the match out.

"We must be near the entrance," Tony said. "Thank goodness for that."

They felt their way past the material, now back on its hook, and to their relief a faint glimmer of light appeared round the next slight bend. Stumbling as quickly as they could over bits of broken rock and stones, they neared the increasing light at the end of the tunnel.

The narrow opening had been roughly covered over with bracken and branches, but these were easily pulled aside and the three were soon standing outside in the open air again.

"Look where we are!" Dip shouted, as he recognised Barton Point in the distance. A strong wind was getting up, blowing now across the marsh; sea birds were crying plaintively and the Welsh hills looked very close.

Now that they were out in the open, their one instinct was to run but Dip, after looking round to make sure they were alone, pulled the bracken and twigs back over the entrance. It was well concealed by the tall spikey grass and gorse bushes nearby. No one ever came to this isolated point of the marsh, not even the bird-watchers. Dangerous channels, looking innocent enough, spread in a network out to the Welsh coast, and covered it completely at high tide. The footpath petered out half a mile away.

Scrambling over the rough grass and running over fields and through a spinney, they arrived back at the bend in Shottington Lane where they stopped to catch their breath.

Bending down to ease the stitch in his side, Dip gasped out "Listen, you two, – don't let's say a word of this to anyone yet. You know what they're like." He remembered bitterly how he'd crossed swords with the sergeant at Weston Police Station, over the episode of the artist. "They'd just say it was nothing – stuff left by a tramp or the Home Guard, or they'd think we made the whole thing up. A spy dressed up as a nun! They'd never stop laughing. Joanna's Dad said there were always false rumours going round, and that's what they'll think it is. But we know that passage is being used for some secretive purpose, and by our spy."

The last bit of Tony's scepticism had vanished. "Yes, Dip's right. We must trap this fake nun ourselves. She, or he," he corrected himself, "won't know we've discovered anything so they won't be suspicious."

"We'll keep guard on the passage. You," Dip turned to Joanna, "watch from your end for anything unusual. And you, Tony, hide yourself by the marsh entrance tomorrow. I'm going to glue myself to old Chiffchaff. That way we're bound to catch someone. We're really onto something, now, I just know we are. We'll meet up at the concert tomorrow and compare notes." His eyes gleamed with excitement. "It's really clever of the person to use that material like a nun's robe – with the convent so near, no one would look twice at another black figure walking along the marsh at dusk or near the church with that old grave of Father Plessey being visited all the time."

"I really thought it was Alice Sayer's ghost down in the tunnel," Joanna said, a little shamefaced, "I was scared to death. It's funny, isn't it, how things link up – Alice's letter, the knot garden pattern and the old chapel and then the passage and those things we found – I wonder . . ." but Dip had forgotten about Alice and the Civil War; his mind was grappling with more recent events. The three went their

117

separate ways after agreeing to absolute secrecy.

As he had no idea of the time, Dip was unprepared for Aunt Mabel's attack as soon as he pushed open the back door. ". . . and I'd even managed to get some liver to make into a stew for supper this evening. Well, we've had ours – the early bird catches the worm." She threw in as a rebuke "Yours is in the oven, and don't blame me if its gone a bit dry by now!"

It had gone rather dry, but Dip ate absentmindedly at one end of the table while Peter was colouring-in a book at the other end.

"Is Chiffchaff around?" he asked casually.

"Yup." Peter didn't look up. His curly head was bent over the gaudy picture of a parrot. Dip noticed he was using his best pre-war crayons – the precious ones with glossy colours on the outside, which were much nicer than the awful pale wooden utility ones they had at school. Peter started chewing the end of the blue one.

"Who said you could use my crayons? Stop biting the end!"

Peter bared his teeth exaggeratedly and closed them over the crayon. Normally, Dip would have sprung at him and there would have been a fight but he didn't rise to the bait this evening. The crayons seemed a trivial matter. Instead, he asked "What's Chiffchaff been doing to-day? Was he bird-watching or digging up someone's rose garden?"

Peter seemed surprised by the mild question. "No, he's in a bit of a bad temper." He lowered his voice – they could hear Aunt Mabel banging around in the kitchen. "He didn't even fancy the stew."

Arthur Finch came down to the sitting room a little later and the four sat in an uneasy silence listening to the news on the wireless.

Dip watched Finch's face closely as reports of bombing and night raids came over, but he remained impassive, puffing away on his pipe. 'How can he sit there so coolly?' Dip wondered. 'I suppose it's their training.'

"Mr Finch, how long do you think the war's going to last?" he asked politely.

"Hard to say," Finch said, not bothering to remove the pipe from his mouth.

"Are you coming to the concert tomorrow evening?"

"Wouldn't miss it." He said this without enthusiasm.

"That reminds me, Dip, just run over my lines with me, would you?" Aunt Mabel produced the script from behind her knitting. "I just can't seem to get them right." She had apparently forgotten her annoyance about the stew and was full of nerves over the thought of the sketch.

"This man needs clean bandages," she pronounced, striking an attitude. There were only six lines to learn but the sequence seemed to elude her. Peter turned away to hide his laughter.

"Now, Dip, you, as prompter must help me if I dry up. I'm relying on you."

She was to be heard all over the house, next day, muttering about 'fresh water' and 'clean bandages'.

Dip slept with his door open that night in case Finch should decide to do some prowling, but he did not hear any sound of padding footsteps. Nor had there been any sign of anyone near the church as darkness fell.

Looking out of his window on Saturday morning, he saw Miss Linniment coming down through the churchyard in earnest conversation with a woman who was a stranger in the village.

"Oh, that'll be Kate Murphy's niece." Aunt Mabel, bringing in a pile of clean clothes, glanced briefly out at the couple. "She looks a respectable body at any rate, not like that aunt of hers."

It could easily be her, Dip was thinking. The Liverpool Irish link was there; but how could she be in two places at once today?

"Miss Linniment has managed to get Kate into the cottage hospital at Weston for a week. She didn't want to go of course; kicked up a terrible fuss apparently, no sense of gratitude. While she's away Miss Linniment and the niece are going to give the cottage a thorough spring clean. They're starting to-day. It's *not* a job I would care for," she added with a sniff.

"What about all the cats?" Dip asked, feeling rather sorry for them, wild and unlovely as they were.

"I have no idea – they'll be turned out, I suppose."

Well, that took care of the niece. If she was spending the day scrubbing and disinfecting under the eagle eye of Miss Linniment she could hardly be down on the marsh, or anywhere else for that matter.

Saturday morning and afternoon passed without incident.

It all seemed a big anticlimax after yesterday and Dip felt depressed and restless.

Arthur Finch hadn't stirred from Dean Farm. He'd helped to shell the peas, sitting on a stool by the large pot of red geraniums, his face turning pink in the hot sun. After lunch of scrap pie, one of Aunt Mabel's own recipes which lived up to it's name, he retired to his room ostensibly to look over some papers, but Dip was sure he was having a nap, as he could hear gentle snores when he went up to the bathroom.

He was despondent, but hoped that at least Joanna would have had better luck. Once again he went over the clues in his mind, when another thought struck him which made him even more disconsolate. Maybe the person, the spy, was someone completely unknown, surfacing only to signal in some way, or vanish off into Liverpool from time to time for information. Maybe he, or she, had been using the passage to live in – perhaps there were two or three hiding places round about where one could stay hidden. A rabbit warren of tunnels, a maze, catacombs. In Dip's mind's eye the Wirral suddenly seethed with subterranean life – underground passages riddled with a network of intercommunicating Nazi headquarters.

Aunt Mabel's voice suddenly roused him from his thoughts. "Just come and hear my lines again, will you?"

Dip groaned.

As they went up to the village hall that evening she was still far from word perfect. Dip tried to reassure her but her usual confidence seemed to have deserted her. She even said dramatically at one stage "I can't go through with it."

Some seats at the back of the hall had been reserved for the Home Guard, who would be coming in late after taking part in a competition at Wirralston. Although it was only half-past seven, several people had already arrived. Mrs Cox was on the door selling tickets, and Dip noticed the Ware-Gillows sitting in the front row and talking loudly to the vicar's sister, who was thanking them for the material they had given for the nuns' costumes.

"Well, we all have to do our bit, that's what I always say." Mrs Ware-Gillow acknowledged the thanks graciously.

Peter was sitting at the side reading a comic; he had obviously forgotten his role as assistant stage manager and was saving the seat next to him for Finch who had still been in the bath when they left.

Behind the curtains and in the dressing rooms the atmosphere was tense with undercurrents of excitement and panic. People were either rushing around looking for things or murmuring lines to themselves in a demented way. Someone was fiddling with the lights, the stage manager was desperately trying to assemble people and organise them into some form of order and one or two people were being very bossy indeed.

"There you are!" Dip found Joanna behind the backdrop, sorting out a variety of equipment for the magic act and keeping a wary eye on the white mice.

"I didn't see *anything* this morning *or* this afternoon," she told him straight away. Dip cautioned her to keep her voice down. "I pretended to be sketching in the garden," she continued in a whisper, "and I even asked if I could have a picnic lunch so I sat quite near the summer house and never saw anything suspicious."

"Nor me," Dip said disconsolately; "perhaps Tony's had some luck."

The hall was filling up – the sound of people's voices talking and laughing made those taking part in the concert even more nervous.

"Going to be a full house." The Reverend Aldous Truce, who was acting as Master of Ceremonies for the evening, beamed as he put his head round the wings. "Oh by the way," he came over to Joanna and Dip and put an arm round each, "I have some news for you two." He dropped his voice confidentially. "Concerning those papers which Mrs Ware-Gillow so kindly let me take away yesterday."

Dip wondered what he would he say if he knew about the passage.

"I must confess," the vicar continued, "that I stayed up half the night reading, it was so interesting. Mrs Sayer did a good deal of research. Apparently poor Sir William died just after the Battle of Rowton Moor in which the Royalists were defeated. He went to Chester to rally round King Charles and was shot by a stray bullet and killed. And that brings me to another interesting point – Alice's friend was a certain Thomas Earnshaw, who was pledged to fight for the Parliamentarians under Sir William Brereton. He fought at Rowton Moor and was presumed killed. Shottington Hall was taken over for a while by the Roundheads and used to house their troops. Imagine what chaos and distress that must have caused. So Alice . . .''

''Come along children, you must *move*.'' A large nun from the chorus bore down on them and the vicar, with some difficulty, returned to the present and realised that he was due to make an announcement in about two minutes. He felt in his pocket for his notes on the concert.

''We'll have another little talk about it some time, shall we?'' he said as he bustled off.

Joanna, who had given the information her rapt attention, said ''I want to know *all* I can.'' But Dip was now looking round for Tony, who still hadn't appeared.

''Now come along please, everybody.'' The distraught stage manager flapped his arms. The noise from the audience suddenly became much quieter as the hall lights went down and the vicar parted the curtains and stepped out in front.

At the same moment, Tony appeared in the wings looking hot and flustered.

''Where on earth have you been?'' Dip hissed at him.

''They wouldn't let me bring Snipe in so I had to leave him by the side door, tied up. He hates it there, but I had to bring him, he's part of the act.''

''Never mind all that – what happened on the marsh – did you see anything?''

''Dead loss,'' Tony shrugged his shoulders. ''Boring, too – I took Grandad's field glasses and hid down by some gorse bushes quite near the passage. But I didn't see a thing.''

A 'wounded Crimean Soldier' gave them a fierce frown.

The vicar had obviously cracked a little joke as the audience responded with a polite laugh and a minute or two later, after some false starts, the curtain swished back and four men including the butcher, wearing false moustaches and boaters, sang a Gilbert and Sullivan selection and then 'Sweet Adeline', which merited an encore.

'The Nuns' Chorus' had been switched to the second half and the sketch was to be the last item before the interval.

The magic act featuring Tony and Joanna was to be performed immediately after the interval.

Peering through the curtains while the small girl was playing her monotonous piece on the piano, Dip saw that Peter was still sitting next to an empty seat.

The music came to an end and all was pandemonium on stage. Makeshift beds were hurriedly assembled and Aunt Mabel in a long skirt and apron clutched Dip on the shoulder. "Remember, I'm *relying* on you," she whispered, fixing him with a fierce look.

Dip felt around for the script and took his place in the wings, concealed by the curtains. He could see Tony and Joanna fussing over an array of brightly coloured scarves, boxes, and large playing cards.

He could also hear Snipe whining outside the hall. He was clearly objecting to having been abandoned there, although the side door was wide open, to let a cool draught of air through the hall on this hot night, and he knew Tony wasn't far away.

At last all was ready. A hush fell over the actors as they took their positions in the ward of Florence Nightingale's hospital.

A scratchy record of Elgar music was played on the wind-up gramophone to set the atmosphere and the curtains were drawn back.

All seemed to be going well until Snipe, aroused by a passing cat or rabbit, set up a series of excited barks.

Sylvia, the landgirl, lying pale and prone in bed, mortally wounded after the Crimea Battle, revived amazingly, and turning to face Dip, glared at him furiously, flapping her arm in an effort to tell him to shut the dog up.

The rest of the cast were looking uneasy as Snipe's continued whining threatened to drown their words, but they pressed on valiantly.

Dip decided he'd better go and find out what was wrong with the dog. As he threw down the script and glanced briefly at the stage, he realised it was almost Aunt Mabel's big moment. He caught the frenzied look in her eye before he rushed down the stairs to sort out Snipe who'd just given a tremendous howl. He intended to smuggle the dog in and be back in time for Aunt Mabel's piece.

"What is it boy?" There was nothing to be seen in the

dusk. All was quiet outside the hall. He glanced round quickly. Then something caught his eye – something so slight that he wondered if he'd imagined it. But no, there it was again – a small shaft of light which flickered briefly in the church window opposite, and then was gone again.

Snipe had quietened down a little so, leaving him tied up, Dip tore across the path, up through the graveyard and round to the vestry door porch. Noiselessly he turned the handle and closing the door behind him, crept into the church.

CHAPTER THIRTEEN

The figure in black

ONCE inside, he stopped, rigid, frozen to the spot, his scalp tingling as he heard once more the chilling, unharmonious but compelling sequence of notes.

Dip drew closer as if guided by some strange force, and then stopped to stand behind a sandstone pillar, listening. There was something evil about the figure – it was certainly not just someone practising. He could only see the back of the black figure but white bony fingers could be seen carefully picking out the notes and Dip was convinced that he should take great care not to be seen or caught.

What should he do? He had no plan. A small hurricane lamp stood by the organ giving a very dim light, and by it he could see what looked like a metal box with wires and an aerial. Suddenly the truth struck him – the strange music was being transmitted. He must fetch help, witnesses. The Home Guard were just across the road at the concert. They would surely know what to do. He must get out as quickly and quietly as he could. But just as he moved, the music stopped.

Had his shoes creaked? Everything was now deathly quiet. The figure at the organ showed no sign of having heard him, but studied a chart resting on the keyboard.

Dip didn't dare move a muscle now; he hardly dared to breathe – and he hoped and prayed that the music would start again so that he could make his escape.

A note sounded once more and he edged cautiously towards the door, but the sound of the note died away and no more followed. Dip was left standing between the pillar and the vestry door.

Very, very slowly and deliberately the black figure half turned and reached for something which was lying by the hurricane lamp. By the light, Dip saw the white hand close over something gleaming and metallic and draw it upwards. To his horror, he recognised it as a Luger automatic. He still hadn't been seen – the only shelter was back behind the pillar. He sensed he must have been heard, but still the person seemed in no hurry – it rose almost in slow motion as if it had all the time in the world and advanced towards the pillar in a leisurely fashion.

He heard the slow, approaching, measured tread coming nearer and nearer and somehow managed to make his own legs move towards the font at the back of the church. The solid mass of stone gave him a little shelter as the relentless footsteps continued but he realised, too late, that by coming to the back of the church he had got himself trapped. The porch door was shut so there was no quick escape that way and the door to the crypt was bolted and would take too long to unfasten. Could he reach the bell tower door?

Now he could even hear the sound of the nun's habit trailing along the stone floor. Quick as lightning, Dip made a bolt for it and reached the small wooden door with a sob of relief; it was ajar. He shoved it open and banged it swiftly again behind him.

He fumbled around, hoping to find a bolt so that he could lock himself in, but there was none. Standing there in the dark, he knew that all he could do was climb the small stone steps upwards and upwards.

For a second, all was quiet. He leant against the stone wall gasping, out of breath with fright, and then the handle of the door slowly turned. Dip watched it in the gloom with dreadful fascination, such as a bird has for a snake about to spring, and then he started to back very cautiously up the stone steps of the spiral staircase.

The door opened inch by inch. Groping his way almost blindly, he turned and forced his legs to continue the steep ascent. He felt crushed into the walls. It was so cramped that it came into his mind that the staircase must have been made for a dwarf.

Up and up he dragged himself. The stone steps were steep.

A tiny arrow slit of a window gave a momentary glimpse of twilight.

He could hear the rustle of the robes below him.

At last he reached the ringing chamber and paused for a brief second to catch his breath. Was there any escape from this level? He remembered the bare, wooden floored room, from the day-time. Here, the bell ropes were looped up, an oak cupboard stood in the corner with the bellringers' instructions pin-ned to it and a large arched window looked over the village and the surrounding Cheshire countryside, but that was all – there was no way out.

He'd have to go on; his legs felt as if they would hardly support him. He'd never been higher than the ringing chamber and wondered where, if anywhere, he would come out. By now he was aching from a stitch in his side and felt his lungs would burst if he had to go much further.

Suddenly, to his horror, he found that he was held fast by his sleeve. He'd been feeling his way up the rough stone walls and his shirt had caught on a nail. Glancing fearfully down, now that his eyes had become accustomed to the dark, he could see the dark shape coming nearer. It was almost at his heels now. It had a face – white and featureless shrouded in black. A pale hand stretched out towards him.

It was like the nightmare he sometimes had, the one where he was running but seemed to stay on the same spot, getting nowhere, while something unknown and menacing threatened to catch up with him. No matter how hard he tried he couldn't move an inch further away. Usually he woke up at this point, but not tonight.

With an almighty tug, he wenched his arm free, with a loud rending sound of cotton, and drew back just before the white hand caught him. Now the walls felt as if they were closing in on him as he scrambled on upwards. The staircase was getting narrower. His heart was thumping; he could hear it beating frantically; and then he heard something else becoming louder and louder as he climbed, tick, tock . . . tick, tock.

With relief he saw that the stairway opened out into another room. It was exactly the same shape as the one below with similar wooden floorboards, but instead of a window, there was a large mechanism ticking away. He realised he was behind the church clock. The bell ropes continued upwards through the floor leading to the bells which hung above.

He could either continue up the steps which wound away out of sight or stay in the clock chamber and face whoever was following him.

He'd have to stop; his legs felt as if they were buckling beneath him. He could hear the figure panting behind. Catching sight of the bell ropes an idea suddenly came to him. He lunged desperately towards the nearest one and tugged it down with all his might. Clang!!

The noise was deafening and vibrated all round the chamber – it felt as if the tower would rock on its foundations, and again it rang – Dong! as it rocked back.

Simultaneously two things happened. From behind the figure following Dip two hairy animals like small lean tigers, with wild screeches propelled themselves past him up the stairs, the one chasing the other, while the figure, which was close to Dip now, crouched and ready to spring, gave a sudden startled cry and fell back, losing its footing on the stairs.

It had all happened so quickly Dip could hardly believe it. There was a muffled thud as the body bumped onto the stone steps below. The bell still reverberated, and then there was silence.

For a minute Dip stood stock still, not daring to go to see what had happened. Perhaps this was the right time to make his escape. Should he hurry down the stairs over the body and make a dash for it out of the church? On the other hand, it might be a trick – this silence – maybe those bony hands were just waiting to grab him.

Very cautiously, he crept onto the narrow staircase again and listened – still no sound – even from the two savage animals who had so miraculously saved him.

Curiosity got the better of him and he edged himself against the wall, descending the steps stealthily.

At the arched entrance to the ringing chamber he saw a black huddled form lying awkwardly on its side. The gun was lying close by.

He could escape now, quickly down the stairs, out of the church and back to fetch help but the figure might revive and vanish for ever, that is – if it was still living and breathing.

He came nearer – who was it? Bending down, he looked more closely, straining his eyes in the dark, and very gingerly reached out and touched the inanimate form. It moved and Dip leapt back, startled. There was a low moan followed by jumbled words in a guttural, foreign language, a man's voice, a hand reached out as if for help.

It didn't sound like Finch and yet . . . Dip picked up the gun and thought quickly. He needed to secure him so that he couldn't get away, but how? The long bell-ropes were looped up nearby – taking hold of the nearest one, Dip uncoiled it and pulled it out to its full length. Not counting the padded piece at the base of the rope, there might just be enough to tie his legs.

While he was figuring out his next move, from high up above, in the church tower, there came the sounds of ominous creaks and shudderings and falling masonry. He glanced up fearfully; something was happening up there and he'd completely forgotten about the bell tower being unsafe.

Instinctively he darted towards the stone arch and steps and pulling and tugging at the groaning man just managed to reach the stairwell before a thunderous crash came from above – it sounded as if the whole church tower was collapsing and then, to his horror, the ceiling of the ringing chamber began to lean inwards, giving way under a tremendous weight, bringing with it crumbling masonry, beams and dust.

One of the great bronze bells had come adrift from the loft, hurtling its way through the floor above and now through the wooden floor of the ringing chamber, down to the porch below, leaving chaos and destruction and a gaping jagged hole where it had fallen. There was a deafening crash as it landed on the hard stone floor beneath. Then there was silence, apart from little falls of stone and splinters.

The white hand by Dip reached out and touched him, making him jump – for a minute he'd forgotten what he was doing there. He looked down at the figure beside him.

"Thank you." The voice was barely audible but Dip managed to make out the words. It was ironic, he thought, that he still didn't know who the person was.

And then from below, he heard the sound of voices and footsteps. Soft light from a torch flickered up through the hole in the floor, followed by shouts of concern and alarm. Up the stone steps the sounds came nearer. The torch shone in Dip's face and he recognised Mr Cox's voice.

"The bell . . . we heard the bell – thought it was the invasion – what the blazes is going on?" Other people crowded into the small space and someone spotted the gun. "What . . . Who's this?"

The torch flashed again and this time lit up the other face. With a shock Dip found himself staring into the defiant eyes of the gardener from Shottington Hall. It was Moses Jones.

Dip started to try and explain, but a cry from a frightened animal overhead was followed by a movement which dislodged a small beam; it swung down and struck him sharply on the head. He didn't remember any more about that night.

CHAPTER FOURTEEN

Safely across the Atlantic

"IT was two of those wild cats – up in the church roof they were and it took the Home Guard all their time to get them down! They must have taken fright when Miss Linniment swept out Kate's cottage! And you should hear Eric Bulley going on about his bell!" Aunt Mabel's voice droned on, outside the bedroom door, to the doctor.

"Just keep him in bed a couple of days – mild concussion and shock – he'll only have a bruise to show for it all by Tuesday."

Dip wriggled his toes between the cool sheets. He didn't see why he couldn't get up now. He'd had quite a few visitors since last night and although they'd been warned not to over-excite him he had been excited. A few gaps had been filled in, in a surprising way.

Arthur Finch, far from being a spy, was working for MI5 under the guise of a man from the Ministry. Suspecting for some time that there was an enemy agent in the area, he had been sent to probe and had found signalling lights on the marsh. He had tried to keep a vigilant watch but had been called away on the very night of the Sealand raid. At the time of the concert he had been down on the marsh, realising that whoever it was would have to give guiding lights again because the fires at the aerodrome had been put out.

Dip had put a stop to that by surprising the intruder in the church and the transmitter set had been found, by the organ.

Moses Jones, which was not his real name of course, had fallen from the sky a few months previously, having been fixed up in a job by his 'cousin' in Liverpool. "From the valleys, he is, you see, terrible leg injury in the mines, but not afraid of hard work.'' Thus they had taken in the Ware-Gillows, who were not ones to miss a bargain – the man had been prepared to work for minimal wages and they had been glad to employ him. His guttural accent was taken for Welsh. It turned out that he had studied Celtic history at Aberystwyth in 1938 – this had probably been a cover while he was engaged in observations for the Germans – and his local knowledge made it reasonably easy to pass himself off as Welsh. Parachuting into an area he was familiar with, he was well situated to infiltrate into the local scene and had managed to pick up snatches of conversations in visits to Dockland pubs. Edwina's boy-friend at Sealand and Joanna's father, a Captain, were added bonuses.

''But what was that strange music I heard? It is still going round and round in my head.''

''The church, you see, being on a rise, made a good place for transmitting,'' Arthur Finch explained. ''The clear notes of the organ would carry well over the air and the code of notes would be impossible to break. He's saying nothing at the moment of course – these Nazi spies know how to keep their mouths shut and when they're cornered they close up like clams – but as far as we can tell, the notes probably refer to points of the compass – a very clever idea. If you can remember the tune, it might help – although it's unlikely they will use anything like it again, once they realise their agent is out of action.'' He smiled.

Dip had been given a lot of praise, even by Aunt Mabel, who forgave him for deserting her in her hour of need. All the same, he felt uncomfortable. He'd been convinced that Finch was the spy and had even suspected that pretty nun from the convent. Those two wild cats darting up the stairs and knocking Moses off balance had probably saved him . . . from what? He shivered. He would never know, but he remembered the gruff ''thank you'' when he pulled Moses free of the crashing bell. The man was human, and perhaps had a family back at home not wanting to be at war any more than Dip's own family. He was being loyal to his own country and putting his life at risk as much as his own father was. But they were on opposing sides. He felt muddled and confused. Joanna was right, he thought, it must have been even worse during the Civil War when members of the same family were fighting each other.

That morning, Tony had been down to the marsh with Arthur Finch to see the signal lights, and had come back feeling sick and angry. He plonked himself down on the bed, crushing Dip's feet.

"It's terrible," he said, his face full of misery. "I saw the guiding light Moses had made – bits of old piping, batteries and two headlamps and guess what? I'm sure one of the headlamps was the one I gave him off Grandpa's old car. He was using our headlamp to guide enemy planes to our own air base."

"Well, you weren't to know, were you?" Dip tried to comfort him. "Anyway, it wasn't used the second time and the first time was just to show the German planes where to start the fires." But Tony was still appalled, and even talk of the concert didn't take the glum look off his face.

Aunt Mabel had completely dried up in the sketch; someone had tried to cover for her but in doing so had ruined the next person's cue. It had taken at least five minutes for the actors to find their parts in the script again and the end of the play, full of dramatic tension, had completely lost its impact owing to the clanging of the church bell and chaos breaking out among the audience.

"We thought it was the invasion – you should have seen the Home Guard – old Cat's-eyes Cox issuing orders and bossing everyone around – no one knew what was happening." Tony managed a slight smile. "Some of the chorus of nuns were furious – they never had a chance to appear after all their hard work and those costumes and now there's talk of fixing another date for a repeat performance."

Clever of Moses to take one of the costumes or some of the material – no one would give him a second glance if they saw him dressed like a nun on the marsh or even round the village in the evening. It must have been silk from *his* parachute and *he* must have dropped the sweet paper.

Dip remembered hearing the whistled tune in Chester and thought back. Yes, he was sure Joanna had told him Moses had taken the Ware-Gillows to Chester that afternoon. He must have had the tune on the brain too and whistled it without thinking that it might be recognised.

They were going over to Shottington Hall the next evening.

Mrs Ware-Gillow had promised one of her chocolate cakes and Joanna's father was coming to hear all the details of the capture and to see the secret passage.

Mr Truce had been excited by the historical significance of the passage leading down to the marsh and he was coming to join the party.

If only Dip could have told the whole story to his parents but he knew he couldn't say anything on the telephone – he'd just have to be patient and wait till he saw them. He found it very difficult.

*   *   *

THE chocolate cake was almost up to pre-war standards and Mrs Ware-Gillow had even produced tit bits from her private store so that cook could make a trifle.

"To think," she kept muttering with her plump hand at her throat, "to think that he was 'ere under our very roof!" she shuddered dramatically. "We could all have been murdered in our beds." The vicar had to console her again.

Captain Palmer listened intently to Dip's story. "It's quite remarkable. The man could have gone undetected for a long time. Let's hope it will make a marked difference to our security in this area, especially with the Atlantic convoys carrying war materials and food getting safely across from America. You've done a grand job, Dip. I shouldn't be surprised if you get some official recognition for this. Now I want to hear all about this passage and how you came to discover it."

Joanna gave a graphic account and they all went outside to the knot garden and saw the design of the old hall and the extra room leading from the library, which had once been the chapel. There were no bonfires today and no sounds of the lawn mower being used.

"I don't mind telling you," Mrs Ware-Gillow confided to Captain Palmer, "I don't know how we're going to cope with this garden – it gives me palpitations just thinking about it."

By the summerhouse they found a bemused looking Mr Ware-Gillow wielding a pair of hedging shears without much confidence. Inside, the deckchairs had been moved and the entrance was now exposed. Arthur Finch had made a brief visit the day before to retrieve the emergency rations and compass left by Moses, who must have come across the tunnel accidently and had kept it to himself, finding it useful for his comings and goings and perhaps as a hideaway in the face of danger.

Joanna and Edwina had discussed the events at length in the kitchen and Edwina was wondering how she could present her own part in it while retelling it to friends. "Of course," she had rehearsed to herself, "I always knew there was something strange about *him*!" In truth, if she had thought of him at all, it had been just as a rather grumpy Welsh gardener.

Joanna remembered his unexpected little gestures of friendship – the offered bitter-tasting chocolate and short, innocent sounding questions about her father that she'd taken for polite interest.

"Oh no, thank you – I'm not going down there. It's bad enough going into the shelter." Mrs Ware-Gillow's hand went up to her hair as if the spiders and bats were already planning an attack.

The others lowered themselves down, aided by a very powerful torch this time, and crept along in single file. When they came to the wider part, where the passage opened out and changed direction, they stopped. The vicar touched the stone walls.

"You know, this was most certainly used to hide away the priests years ago when they were persecuted. If the present library was the chapel and there was an ante-room where the summerhouse now stands, there was probably a false floor board there; it would have been covered by a rug concealing the entrance so the priest could hide in here or escape down to the estuary, if, as you say, this passage leads to the marsh."

Joanna sat on a rough stone seat cut from the sandstone and tried to imagine it all.

"He would probably have taken some food and maybe some books to read while he waited. Books written in Latin, I expect, and he'd have had to put his candles up on the ledge." She stood on the seat and looked into the deep recess cut into the wall behind the jutting, narrow piece of rock which served as a long shelf.

"He'd have had room here to put . . ." Joanna had put her hand in the recess to prove her point and withdrew it sharply with a cry. "Ugh! I felt something in there – a dead rat or something!" She screwed up her face in horror. Her father raised the torch and shone the beam onto something dark and leathery at the back.

"Let's have a look." He reached in and pulled out a bundle that looked like a pouch or a purse. It was very ancient, the leather cracked and stiff. It was about eight inches long.

"Is it something Moses Jones left behind, do you think?" Dip asked.

"No, I should think this has been here for a good many years longer than that. It's not a rat, anyway."

The vicar took it and examined it with avid interest. "I've seen something like this before in a very old house in Warwickshire, which is open to the public. It must be two or three hundred years old, I should say!"

His enthusiasm was boyish and now that she knew it wasn't a dead rat or a bat, Joanna became excited too. "Can we open it?"

The vicar's hands were shaking as he opened up the stiff leather while the others crowded round, not knowing what he would discover.

"You found it – you look inside," he said to Joanna.

She still felt a bit squeamish as she put her hand into it. Her fingers closed round something smooth and stiff. "It's a piece of parchment – oh hang on, there's something else as well." She handed the parchment to the vicar and delved round inside again. "Look!" she exclaimed with triumph and held up a jewel which glistened in the light from the torch. It was a cross in which were set bright red stones and diamonds which twinkled and sparkled. The chain which held it was gold and interspersed with beads.

Joanna had seen similar ones at the convent. "It's a rosary isn't it?" she asked Mr Truce, who nodded.

"A very special one by the looks of it!"

She fingered the cross tenderly and suddenly the portrait of Alice Sayer flashed through her mind. *She* was holding a rosary just like this – could it possibly be the same one?

"The portrait," she blurted out, "upstairs!" The others knew the one she meant but they hadn't studied it closely enough to know if it was the same rosary.

"We'll go straight back and compare it. It will be quite amazing if it *is* the same." Captain Palmer smiled at his daughter. "To think of it lying here all those years – however do you suppose it came to be here?"

The vicar, meanwhile, had been looking more closely at the piece of parchment. "There's a seal on the other side – it isn't just a blank piece of parchment – it's folded, like a letter." A small piece of red sealing wax held the fold together, as it had held it for nearly three hundred years.

In the drawing room, the others could hardly contain their impatience while Dip went to find Mr and Mrs Ware-Gillow. This was their property, after all.

Joanna couldn't wait another second – she raced upstairs to examine the portrait of Alice. It *was* the same rosary, she'd been sure of it, and there was the knot garden in the background, showing the design of her house.

The Ware-Gillows had been assembled by the time Joanna rushed back.

"I don't know what all this fuss is about I'm sure," Mrs Ware-Gillow said, but she admired the cross and pronounced the red stones to be real rubies, with an experienced eye. Mr Ware-Gillow, glad to have been called away from the arduous task of trying to clip a hedge, had settled himself down in his comfortable wing armchair, his eyes heavy lidded, looking as if they might close at any minute.

The vicar broke the seal while everyone watched expectantly. Joanna craned her neck to see more clearly. There was indeed writing on the page, small writing in the familiar brown ink.

He fumbled in a pocket for his reading glasses and it seemed an age before he settled them on his nose – Joanna felt like screaming. He studied the page for a minute or two and sat down on the nearest chair, looking up at them all, his eyes shining.

"Do you know, I believe this will solve the mystery of what became of Alice Sayer. You will have to bear with me – it is written in seventeenth century English but I will do my best."

Slowly and carefully the Reverend Aldous Truce read out the words written so long ago.

My dearest Cousin,

Such misfortune has fallen on us of late.

My father, joining the King in the besieged city of Chester was shot by a stray bullet soon after our defeat at Rowton Moor. How long the city can withhold the might of the Parliamentarians, I know not, I beg you to pray for the departed soul of my father for he died of his wound.

It was his wish that I should enter the Convent of the Blessed Mary but this will never now be.

Four days since, the very night before I should have retired from the outside world and taken my final vows in France, there was a great clamour in the courtyard. All the men at the Hall are gone to the War. I hastened down . . . it was Thomas Earnshaw, sorely injured after the battle, near to falling from his horse.

I did hide him in our secret cave and did tend his wounds with my trusted Deb, who guarded.

His health improves daily, thank God and two days hence we will come through the Priests' passage to the estuary and thence to Ireland and a ship to a new life in Virginia where we will be man and wife. In a new country at peace from this most terrible conflict.

Dearest cousin, in renouncing the religious life, I send you my rosary – pray for us. I prithee reward Deb for her loyalty to our family.

Remember me
Your devoted Cousin Alice

They were all quiet for a moment, then Joanna said "Virginia, that's in America, isn't it? They went to America and were married; perhaps they had children and maybe there's someone alive *now* who's a direct descendant."

"It's quite possible," Mr Truce said.

"And it's also quite possible that a Sayer descendant of theirs will come over with the American forces to help us fight in *this* war," Joanna's father said.

"But why was the letter left in the passage – why wasn't it delivered?" Dip asked.

"Well," the vicar paused; "there are one or two probable explanations. I told you that the Hall was taken over soon after the battle by Roundheads. It would have been overrun with soldiers – perhaps Deb fled back to her home and safety and of course there was a fearful epidemic of the plague shortly after that time and . . . but we won't dwell on that; this is a happy occasion, one for celebration.''

Mrs Ware-Gillow pricked up her ears at the word celebration and went off to get her decanter of pre-war Amontillado sherry, muttering ''I've never known a week like it!''

While the vicar exclaimed again at his delight at the find and assured everyone that the rosary would be placed in safe keeping and a possible search for a member of the family instigated as soon as possible, the children crept away. Joanna, after arranging to meet the boys at the weekend for a further and very necessary rehearsal of Tony's magic act, was eager to find Edwina and tell her about the happy ending to Alice's story. She knew Edwina would be thrilled; 'just like the ending of a film!' she'd probably say. She still could hardly believe it herself. Looking at the portrait, she'd always feel a surge of pleasure and happiness now. How funny that Francesca Stewart had inadvertently been the one to give them the clue about the knot garden – even *she* wasn't so bad these days – she'd actually asked Joanna to partner her in the tennis tournament. It would be the end of term before very long; she'd come second in a history test and there was a short holiday to look forward to with her father . . . she sighed contentedly.

Edwina was sitting at the kitchen table hulling some strawberries and she looked up and smiled as Joanna came in.

*　　　*　　　*

THE two boys passed by the knot garden – fragrant with the scent of mint, lavender, rosemary and other herbs, peaceful, serene and timeless, unchanged through all the different scenes it had witnessed.

''I bet the vicar couldn't believe his eyes when he saw the mess the bell made crashing down to the porch!'' Tony laughed.

''I suppose it'll take ages to get it all put right. Those cats . . .'' He broke off sharply and clutched Tony's sleeve. ''Did you see that?''

Tony nodded and stared where a trail of black fabric suddenly disappeared behind a rhododendron bush. "Oh *no* – not another nun." But it turned out to be only Miss Linnament, weighed down by a number of costumes from the concert performance, which she hoped Miss Jardine might keep in one of the attics until the next presentation of the show.

"Oh – David – I was hoping to see you. Your Aunt Mabel said you were here." Her voice seemed more mellow and patient than it usually was when speaking to him. "A very worthwhile effort of yours . . . most praiseworthy," she said vaguely, "and I have a message from your Aunt – now, let me see – oh yes . . . your mother rang this afternoon. She will be home tomorrow night and your father will be coming too for two or three days' convalescence. Now, won't that be nice?"

Nice! It would be wonderful! Dip could hardly believe his ears. He took hold of Miss Linniment and whirled her around until she was dizzy. "Stop, stop, that's enough now," she protested, and put out a hand to steady herself.

"I suppose you'll be pleased to hear too," she went on when she'd regained her breath, "that those two wild cats have been safely brought down from the tower – and what a hazardous exploit that was – managed supremely well by our own Home Guard. After all their – er – fleas have been exterminated, and they have had full medical attention – they will be allowed to return to live with Kate Murphy and her niece in their cottage which is as clean as a new pin now," she ended triumphantly.

Dip was hardly listening. With Arthur Finch back in London, his mission completed, and his parents both home – even if his father's stay was only to be brief, things would almost seem normal again. Almost, but not quite; nothing would be *exactly* right until after the war. He would just enjoy these few days as much as possible, live in the present and relish every moment.

"Now, where can I find Mrs Ware-Gillow? I have a most important message for her too," Miss Linniment said in her old brisk style. "I have just heard that a large group of children from the East End of London will be arriving by train on Thursday and places have to be found for them all at very short notice. I am hopeful that Mrs Ware-Gillow will be able to accommodate at least a dozen. After all, the Hall *is* very large." Her voice faltered slightly.

Visions rose up before the boys' eyes – beautiful visions of rapturous summer holidays spent stalking, making dens, poaching, fighting, trailing – just like the Arcadian time they'd had with the boys from Bootle.

"Oh, yes," Dip said earnestly, trying to look serious. "I'm *sure* Mrs Ware-Gillow will be very pleased to have them; she's always saying we all have to do our bit!"